She feathered kisses on the corners of his carved mouth. "Now why would you want to do something like that?" she asked softly.

Rafael smiled and kissed her. "I said nothing about *wanting*," he said. "I'm going to be in a charity bullfight."

Analisa's back stiffened. "Bullfight? But why? I think that's terrible and thoughtless of you to do that now that you are married! You could be killed!"

"Nothing is going to happen to me, *querida*." He traced the delicate line of her cheek.

BRITTANY YOUNG

decided to write romances when she found herself living one. She describes her courtship as being as dramatic as our love stories, and her husband as the quintessential Silhouette hero. Her interests include drawing, music, photography and history. An accomplished linguist, she can say "I love you" in perfectly accented French, Spanish and Greek.

Dear Reader:

I'd like to take this opportunity to thank you for all your support and encouragement of Silhouette Romances.

Many of you write in regularly, telling us what you like best about Silhouette, which authors are your favorites. This is a tremendous help to us as we strive to publish the best contemporary romances possible.

All the romances from Silhouette Books are for you, so enjoy this book and the many stories to come. I hope you'll continue to share your thoughts with us, and invite you to write to us at the address below:

Karen Solem
Editor-in-Chief
Silhouette Books
P.O. Box 769
New York, N.Y. 10019

BRITTANY YOUNG
Arranged Marriage

Silhouette *Romance*

Published by Silhouette Books New York

America's Publisher of Contemporary Romance

 SILHOUETTE BOOKS, a Simon & Schuster Division of
GULF & WESTERN CORPORATION
1230 Avenue of the Americas, New York, N.Y. 10020

ISBN: 0-671-57165-6

First Silhouette Books printing July, 1982

10 9 8 7 6 5 4 3 2 1

Arranged
Marriage

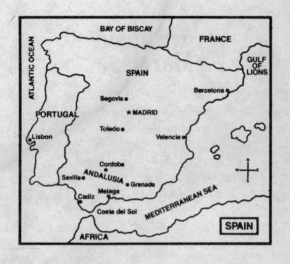

Chapter One

To the old doctor who had known the dying man in the bed and the beautiful blonde girl seated next to him, the scene was heartrending. The girl looked up at him, her emerald eyes hollow with grief, yet with just a spark of hope that the doctor would give her some sign her father would be all right. He shook his head sadly.

Analisa Durant looked back at the prone figure of her father, once such a strong man, now emaciated and broken in his old age, and wanted to cry out with the undeniable pain of losing him. He had married late in his life. Analisa had been born when he was already in his fifties, at the cost of his wife's life. Ever since she could remember, it had just been the two of them here on the estate. Tears sparkled on her long, dark lashes, but she hastily wiped them away with the back of her hand and put on a shaky smile when Marcus Durant opened his eyes and looked up at her.

"Hello, Sunshine," he whispered hoarsely, using the name he had bestowed on her as a child. "It's time for us to have that talk now."

"No, daddy, not now, please." She reached out

and covered one of his wrinkled hands with both of her smooth ones. "You have to rest, conserve your strength."

The man weakly shook his white head. "Resting isn't going to help and we both know it, right Maxwell?" He looked up at the doctor who moved immediately to his side.

"Since you insist on giving everyone such a rough time, I guess we'll never know," the old doctor said gruffly.

"Ah, bah!" Marcus grunted with a spark of his old self, turning back to his daughter. Her future fate was his main concern, now that he wasn't going to be here to guide her. "Do you remember a while back when we had that talk about Rafael Santiago?"

Analisa nodded. "The eldest son of your dearest friend. I remember, but I really don't think . . ."

"Please, let me finish." He patted her hand, and his eyes, so much like his daughter's, got a faraway look in them. "It was back in the thirties, during all the furor of the Spanish Revolution. José Santiago and I met. He saved my life, you know."

"I know, daddy. You told me all about it. He took a bullet that was meant for you."

"That's right. And I never forgot. He was the best friend a man could ask for. Still is, for that matter, even though he lives in Spain." The faraway look left his eyes and he focused on this beautiful golden child he and his beloved wife had brought into this world at such a huge price. "What I didn't tell you about our friendship is that we pledged his eldest son, and my eldest daughter. You weren't even born yet—nor was the young Santiago."

Analisa looked at her father with something akin

to horror on her face. "Pledged? You don't mean you betrothed me to someone without my knowledge!"

."That's exactly what I mean to tell you." His voice was getting weaker. Emerson has the details and the agreement, drawn up over fifty years ago." Emerson Langford was the family lawyer and dear, dear friend. He was like an uncle to Analisa—and, in fact, she called him by that title.

But right now, she couldn't believe what she was hearing. Her father had chosen a husband for her without her knowledge or consent!

Marcus Durant gave a tired chuckle. "I remember when José and Rafael came to visit us all those years ago. You were a gangling ten-year-old, and Rafael was a tall, handsome twenty-three. You developed the most intense crush on him. Both José and I were well pleased with our work that day."

Analisa remembered that visit all too well. Rafael had been her first love. And most painful. She had disdained boys up to that point, preferring to climb trees and play baseball. Then Rafael came to stay with them for a week, along with his father. He was unlike anyone she had ever met, with hair black as a raven's wing, and dark skin. His eyes had come as a surprise, as blue as the Mediterranean, with always a sparkle of humor in their depths. She had taken one look at him and retired her baseball mitt to the top shelf of the closet and turned in her jeans for dresses. She still blushed to think of what a complete fool she had made of herself, following him everywhere, demanding attention and being crushed when he focused it elsewhere, which inevitably happened.

The daughter of one of their neighbors was a buxom eighteen-year-old, and once Rafael had gotten a look at her, he didn't have time to bother with the little ten-year-old with the wistful green eyes. It was then that she realized that any attention he had given her before that was simply because he felt sorry for her and didn't want to hurt her feelings.

On the last day of his visit, he had, with Marcus Durant's permission, invited the buxom Lucy to dinner. Analisa, who had put on her prettiest dress for the occasion, and curled her hair, was so outraged at this slight that she promptly walked up to him and kicked him soundly in the shin; then she had run up to her room and refused to come out again.

When the pounding on her door stopped, she thought everyone had decided to leave her alone. She was wrong. Rafael climbed the rose trellis to her second-story bedroom and came in the window. She hadn't seen him come in and could still remember the stunned surprise she had felt when his hand had grabbed her by the shoulder and swung her over his knee. He then proceeded to administer her very first spanking. Her father had never touched her in anger.

When he had finished, Analisa could remember standing there glaring at him furiously and rubbing her rear end. Rafael was coldly furious. "You will go down there and apologize to Lucy at once," he informed her.

"I will not!" she shot back. "And when my father finds out what you just did, *you'll* be the one doing the apologizing!" She was close to tears but was determined not to let the Spaniard know.

His deep, slightly accented voice was a study in coolness. "On the contrary, little witch, I have your father's permission."

Her mouth opened in disbelief. How could her father have done something like that! Quickly she thought about her options. If she didn't apologize, she was in for another spanking, and she was most certainly not going to apologize. That meant the only thing she could do was make a run for it. She backed toward the door, trying to look nonchalant, then made a mad dash, but she couldn't get it unlocked before Rafael had her over his knee again.

"This is going to hurt me more than it is you, little one, but it is a matter of pride." And with that he administered two firm spanks.

This time tears of rage made it to her eyes and she quickly brushed them away with the back of her hand. Her pride had been hurt much more than her bottom.

Rafael had risen and picked up a handkerchief from her dresser. Then he had crossed back to her and wiped her eyes, gently smoothed her hair and held his arm out to her. "And now we will return to the dining room where you will apologize and eat your dinner along with everyone else. Is that understood?"

Without another word, but seething with resentment, she did as he bid. Thus ended her infatuation with the Spaniard . . . or so she thought. It was strange how, even now, she could remember exactly what he looked like.

But, she was twenty-three now, and bore little resemblance to that besotted ten-year-old. She was a teacher, and a good one, and didn't want to marry anyone until she fell in love. Her thoughts brought her back to the present. "Father," she said, keeping her voice soft, "you aren't serious about this, are you?"

He sighed. "I knew you'd be shocked. I so wanted to break it to you differently. Little did I know there wouldn't be time."

"Don't say that!" She managed to put a smile into her voice. "We'll have lots of time to argue about this!"

He winked at her but didn't comment.

The old doctor held his patient's wrist between his fingers thoughtfully for a moment, then placed it back on the cover. "Marcus, I'm going to have to ask you to stop talking now. You aren't doing yourself any favors." He looked over at the girl. "Analisa, I'm afraid I'm going to have to ask you to leave."

"No!" Her father grabbed her hand as she began to rise. "Sunshine, you have to promise me," he said breathlessly, "that you'll marry Rafael Santiago if he'll have you, just as José and I planned. "Promise me!"

"But, daddy . . ."

"I'd never ask you to do anything that might hurt you. Trust me in this."

"But what if he doesn't want me?" she asked in desperation.

"Then you're free from the promise. But I want your word that if he'll have you, you'll marry him. Promise me, or I'll never be able to rest easily. Please."

"All right, daddy, all right. Don't get excited. I'll

do as you ask." She took his hand and held it briefly to her lips before placing it back on the sheet. "Don't worry about me anymore, all right?"

With that, Marcus Durant lay back onto his pillows with a sigh of relief and a smile, and drifted quietly into death.

Chapter Two

Weeks later, long golden hair shimmering down her back, her tanned shoulders left bare by the strapless green sundress she wore, she kicked off her sandals and began running as fast as she could across the small Vermont estate where she and her father had lived for as long as she could remember. Hot tears streamed down her cheeks in a suddenly unleashed torrent of grief. She had held herself in check all this time, but now the estate was going to be sold to pay some outstanding debts, and memories of the wonderful times here had filled her heart to the breaking point. So intent was she on her flight that she didn't see the foreign sports car coming down the drive or the tall, dark man who emerged from it.

She flew over the manicured lawn with the grace of a wild creature, and up a grassy knoll to the little pond where she and her father had fished on lazy warm days like today. She used to sit here by the hour and dream . . . about knights and kings, and things to come.

But now she stood there pulling air painfully into her burning lungs. She sat on the ground, unaware of the beauty of the sunshine, unaware of its warmth. She rolled onto her stomach, resting her forehead on folded arms, and cried as though her heart was breaking. Everything in her life was changing so quickly. First the death of her father, then the sale of the only home she had ever known, and soon she would have to travel to Spain to see if a man she hadn't seen for thirteen years would marry her.

A gentle hand touched her shoulder and a deep, slightly accented voice said softly, "Analisa."

She twisted into a sitting position, her glorious eyes surrounded by long dark lashes spiked with tears, and looked up at the tall Spaniard. He was older looking now, his handsome features appearing even more darkly carved. Her breath caught in her throat. For just a fraction of a second, so quickly that she hardly noticed it come and go, she reverted to that ten-year-old who had loved him. But then she remembered their last meeting. "What are you doing here?"

He looked arrogantly down at her. "I should think that would be obvious."

The last thing she wanted to do was cry in front of him, but she couldn't seem to stem the flow of tears long enough to express the anger she felt at this unwanted intrusion. "Just go away, please. I don't want you here." Her voice was a hoarse whisper. "My father . . ."

After a slight hesitation, he gathered her stiffly resisting form into his strong arms with a sigh. "I know. That's why I'm here."

Her cheek was against the cool material of his sport coat and her tears still streamed. She stopped resisting. It was so much easier just to lean on him. He removed one arm from around her long enough to hand her a snowy white linen handkerchief, then smoothed her hair with a comforting hand. "Cry, *querida*. Cry until it hurts no more," he told her quietly.

And she did, until her tears were all used up and only dry sobs racked her slender body. Rafael lifted her away from him, taking the handkerchief and drying her tears himself. "Better?"

She nodded in embarrassment and looked away, remembering another time when he had wiped away her tears. "I'm sorry. This must be very trying for you."

He shrugged his broad shoulders. "It is a woman's prerogative to cry. Like changing her mind."

Analisa forgot about her father for a moment, and her shoulders straightened noticeably, causing the grooves in the Spaniard's cheeks to deepen. "That's a myth put about by male chauvinists like yourself!"

He inclined his dark head, obviously unconvinced. "As you wish." He changed the subject. "I would have been here sooner, but my father, too, fell ill. He is all right now," he assured at her look of distress, "but it was close."

"I'm glad he's all right. I remember him well from your visit. He's a charming man." Unlike his eldest son, she privately thought. She raised her green eyes to Rafael's and got the strangest feeling he knew exactly what she was thinking.

"Ah, yes. Our visit. That bruise you gave me lasted for a month."

Analisa's cheeks grew pink. "I was hoping you'd forgotten about that. All of that."

A corner of his shapely mouth lifted. "Not a

chance." He looked out over the lazy pond. "I understand you are putting the estate up for sale."

She looked at him suspiciously. "How did you know that?"

Rafael took off his sport coat and laid it on the grass beside him, leaning back on an elbow. "I had a talk with your Mr. Langford this morning on my arrival."

Analisa was immediately back on the defensive. "Oh! You had no right! This is none of your affair!"

"On the contrary, it is very much my affair. I understand you now know about our betrothal."

Her eyes widened. "You mean you know also? When did you find out?"

"I was told about it the day you were born."

"Then you knew what they intended for us when you visited!"

"Our betrothal, little one, was the reason for the visit. My father had the hope that if I met you, I wouldn't be so rebellious."

Analisa couldn't help the impish smile which lit her lovely face. "I imagine you were just thrilled to death with the situation by the time you left."

Rafael threw back his head and laughed, a rich, warm sound. "You might say that." His blue eyes became serious. "How do you feel about things?"

Her smile faded and she rubbed her forehead tiredly. "To tell you the truth, I can't believe this is happening. I have a good job, friends, my horse, my home . . . or at least I used to have my home. My whole life is here, and it's being turned upside down and there's nothing I can do about it."

"Don't be so sure." He rose to his feet and pulled

her up also. "I have some matters to attend to in town, papers to go over with your attorney, but I would like to have dinner with you this evening. We can discuss a solution to our dilemma. You may believe me when I say I have no more wish to marry you under these circumstances than you have to marry me."

Curiously, Analisa felt insulted, even though what he said was true. Perhaps it was just the way he said it. "All right. But what if we can't find a solution?"

Rafael picked up his sport coat and flung it over his left shoulder, hooking it on a finger. Then he took Analisa's hand in his free one as they began the walk back to the house. "Then the next forty years are going to be painfully long for both of us."

She took special care with her appearance that evening, braiding her long hair and winding it around her head Scandinavian style. The dress she chose was one of her favorites, white with off-the-shoulder puffed sleeves reaching to her finely boned wrists. The neckline was gathered peasant style, becoming slim-fitting at her narrow waist and flaring into a full skirt that reached to just below her knees.

For jewelry, all she wore was a gold-link belt and delicate gold earrings in her pierced ears. Her emerald eyes needed no makeup, being naturally dark-lashed and browed, and her skin was still tanned enough to show off to advantage without cosmetics. At the sound of the doorbell, she put on a dash of rose-colored lipstick, and with a breathless smile she ran down the carpeted stairs of the cozy Tudor house to open the front door.

He studied her silently, from the toes of her

golden sandals to the top of her braided head. "I can see that I shall be the envy of every man in the restaurant this evening."

Analisa had, in the meantime, been doing her own studying. Rafael had dressed in a three-piece black suit with a crisp white shirt opened at the collar, allowing a glimpse of strong, tanned throat. His blatant animal magnetism took her breath away—much against her will. "I have a feeling the women in the restaurant won't be far behind," she quipped, causing Rafael to laugh.

An unspoken truce had been established. The embers of resentment were still smoldering just below the surface, however, and ready to burst into flame at the slightest provocation.

She picked up the clutch bag she had placed on the hall table while Rafael watched approvingly. "Not only beautiful, but on time. A rare combination at best. Shall we?" He led her out of the house, locking the door behind them, and tucked her comfortably into the passenger seat of his Jaguar, then folded his own long frame into the driver's side.

After several minutes of companionable silence in the fast moving car, Rafael looked over at her. "How are you feeling?"

She smiled at him gratefully. "Much, much better. I guess I really did need to cry the grief out of my system. I don't quite know how to describe it," she said thoughtfully, but somehow . . . while I still miss my father, and I know I always will, the pain associated with thinking about him is gone."

He threw the car into a lower gear as they reached the traffic of the city. His driving was superb. "That is good. It means your wounds are healing. Do you feel any better about selling the estate? And your horse?"

Analisa shook her head. "No. I love that old house, and Pippa. Selling them will be like selling a part of myself." She looked out at the passing traffic. "I'd give anything if I could keep them, but there's the rather large matter of paying for father's medical and hospital bills. The only way I can do it is to sell."

The powerful automobile was stopped at a red light and Rafael looked over at her in the darkened car. "I could pay those for you, you know."

Analisa shook her golden head. "Thank you, but no. The debts are my responsibility, and I'd like to take care of them myself."

The light changed and he put the car into gear. "As you wish."

He skillfully parked the car in front of a small Italian restaurant that she had never been to before.

He opened the car door and helped her out. "How did you know I like Italian food?" she asked smilingly.

"Everyone likes Italian food, but as it turns out, I chose this place more because of atmosphere than cuisine."

She soon found out what he meant. It was rather dark, and while there seemed to be a lot of people, it was surprisingly quiet and restful, conducive to conversation. The maître d' recognized Rafael and with a word of greeting, led them to a back table, lit only by the glow of candlelight.

Rafael ordered wine and dinner for the two of them, without consulting her, then relaxed in his chair. "So, what do you think?"

"It's nice," she told him sincerely, repressing the

annoyance she felt about not being asked what she wanted to eat. "I never even knew it was here. How did you find it?"

His blue eyes studied her thoughtfully. "I knew we'd need to do some talking, so I went for a walk this afternoon to check out a couple of restaurants. This is the one I liked."

"So do I." She smiled.

"That's one thing we have in common, then. What else do you suppose there is?" His tone suggested that he personally thought that was the end of the road for compatibility. Again she felt her hackles rising, but before she could respond, the wine arrived and he raised his glass in a toast. "To your beauty and your future happiness."

Analisa blushed at the unexpected compliment. "Thank you. To your happiness also."

He inclined his dark head and they both drank. She was amazed at what good company he could be when he chose.

"Tell me about yourself, Analisa Durant," he said suddenly. "What has your life been like?"

She put down her wine and shrugged her shoulders. "Not very exciting, but happy enough. I never knew my mother. She died when I was born. Father raised me alone until I was ten, then sent me to a boarding school where I learned the finer points of being a lady. From there I went on to four years of college in Vermont and lived at home while I got my teaching degree. For the past year I've been a teacher at an elementary school—or at least I was until the summer break started last week."

"I see." He stared into his glass of red wine. "You made no mention of men, yet you have the look of a woman who would attract many. Have you ever been in love?"

Analisa leaned forward, looking into her own wine, unaware of the attractive picture she made with the candlelight glistening on her golden shoulders. "I don't think so—which probably means no. I rather imagine when one is in love, one knows it."

Rafael looked at her with intense blue eyes. "One knows it," he said succinctly.

She looked at him curiously. "What about you? The last time we met, you were in the process of becoming an architect."

"I have my own firm in Madrid."

She couldn't help but think that he didn't really look like an architect. He looked as though he would be involved in something riskier than that. Something where he was defying death all the time. There was a certain something behind his eyes. A hardness. A cynicism that said he had done it all. An aloofness which proclaimed him untouchable by mere human emotions.

"And have you"—she looked at him hesitantly—". . . have you ever been in love?"

He looked at her over the rim of his wineglass. "I have had many loves in my life. After all, I'm thirty-six years old. But only one true love."

Analisa felt a knot grow in her stomach. For reasons which she herself hadn't the experience or wisdom to understand, it bothered her that a woman had been able to get that close to him.

"I think you will like my family," he continued as their dinner was served. "You have already met my father, of course, although he has become frail since the last time you saw him. And in his home live my sister Julia, my younger brother Manuel, my father's sister, Tía Maria, who runs his home, and my sister's fiancé, Jaime. He both lives on the ranch and works there."

"It sounds a busy place compared to what I'm used to." The dinner was delicious, but when was Italian food not? Analisa looked around the restaurant at one point, and was amused to see that she had been right. The women were craning their necks to get a better look at Rafael. She didn't notice that the men were doing the same thing to her.

With dinner finished, they sat at the table in silence, sipping cognac and coffee. "So," she finally said. "You haven't told me how we're going to solve our problem yet."

"No, I haven't. Under normal circumstances there would be no problem. I informed my father when first told about our betrothal that I would not accept an arranged marriage with anyone. I wanted to be free to choose my bride."

Analisa sighed. "I'm so sorry. I seem to be causing you a lot of trouble." A thought struck her and she looked at him, suddenly hopeful. "My father told me that I only had to marry you if you were willing. Since you aren't, I'm free from my promise!"

"Not quite." He dashed her hopes to the ground. "You see, my father, as I mentioned, is a very old, very frail man. The last illness I told you about was a heart attack. Any stress could bring on another, fatal one. So, when he asked me to come here to help you out after your father's death and bring you back as my fiancée, I could only agree."

He hadn't come here because he wanted to help

23

her out himself, she thought. "What you're saying then, is that we must pretend to be engaged until your father is strong enough to handle the truth?"

"Exactly. Are you willing to help me out in this?"

Her eyes studied his chisled mouth and moved slowly to his eyes. "Do you mind if I ask you a question?"

He raised a black brow. "I won't know that until you ask, will I?"

She ignored his irony. The wine and cognac were making her more forward than she was normally. She wasn't used to drinking at all. "Where did you get those incredible blue eyes of yours?"

He smiled at her, seeming to realize she was tipsy. "My father's first wife, my mother, was an English-woman."

"Do your brother and sister have blue eyes also?"

"They are a product of my father's second marriage to a Spanish woman, so no, they don't."

"I see." She let out a long breath. "Yes."

"I beg your pardon?"

"Yes. I'll pretend we're engaged—for your father's sake, of course."

He smiled at her. "Of course." Then he removed a small black box from his suit coat pocket and set it before her. "Since we are to be officially engaged shortly, I thought this would be appropriate. I hope you like it, Analisa."

The sound of her name on his lips sent a shiver of pleasure down her spine. The way he lightly accented it made it sound lovelier than it was, and her more dear.

She looked first at the box, then at him, then back at the box.

"Go ahead," he encouraged. "Open it."

She picked it up slowly and raised the lid. Lying on a bed of black velvet was a band, a delicate band, encrusted with diamonds and emeralds in single file all the way around. It was an antique, and obviously of great value. "I can't," she gasped, only to be silenced by Rafael.

"Please. If you don't like it, I will take it away. If you do, then say nothing, but wear it."

When she still hesitated he took it from the box himself and placed it gently on her ring finger. Perhaps it was an omen. The fit was perfect.

She looked at her hand, then held it out for his inspection. He took it firmly in his and kissed the ring. "It suits you, Analisa Durant." His blue eyes met hers with a message she didn't dare interpret.

The drive home was accomplished in companionable silence. Analisa was so relaxed and happy that she was disappointed when they pulled into her driveway. He helped her out of the car and, arm in arm, they walked to the door.

"Would you like to come in for some coffee?" she offered, hoping against hope that the evening wasn't over quite yet.

"I don't think so." He took the keys from her and opened the door. "Sweet dreams, little witch," he said softly, kissing her forehead and walking back to his car.

She watched him drive off, feeling somewhat dreamy. This she attributed to the wine. That night she slept with her left hand under her cheek where she could feel the ring Rafael had given her.

This she attributed to . . . well, this she tried not to think about.

Chapter Three

Early the next bright spring morning, the doorbell rang. Analisa, who had been cleaning, ran to answer it and smiled at the old man standing there. "Hi, Uncle Em! I wasn't expecting you."

The attorney gave her long ponytail an affectionate tug. "I know, dear. I tried to call you last night, but no one answered."

"I was out with Rafael," she explained, closing the door behind her uncle and taking him into the sunny living room. "Did you want to see me about a legal matter, or is this strictly a friendly visit?"

"Both." He sat down on the long white couch with a tired sigh. "But before I go into the business end of it, do you have some coffee an old man could wet his whistle with?"

"Of course." She started for the kitchen. "And I'll even go you one better. How does a nice, big, fresh-from-the-oven chocolate chip cookie sound?"

"Ah, my one weakness and she goes right for it! Haven't had a home-baked chocolate chip cookie since the last time I was here."

She returned in a matter of minutes with a tray and watched his brow furrow as she poured the coffee and served him. Then she sat next to him and patted his suited knee. "Come on, Uncle Em. It can't be all that bad. What's the matter?"

He took a bite of cookie then looked directly into her eyes. "I sold the property this morning. The house and everything."

Analisa's breath left her in a gasp. "So soon? But we hadn't even put it on the market yet. I thought it would take months. . . ."

"I know. So did I. But the gentleman I sold it to heard about it and offered us more than we would have asked. It will take care of all the bills. I couldn't turn it down."

"No, no, of course not," she reassured him distractedly. "They have to be paid." She was really shaken. Before, the selling of the estate was always in the background of her thoughts, but now it was a reality, and a painful one. She cleared her throat, trying to avoid the tears that were so close. "Who bought it? Anyone we know?"

"I'm afraid he wants to remain anonymous, dear. It's to be a surprise for someone and he doesn't want there to be any chance of word leaking out beforehand."

"I see." She walked over to the French-paned windows and looked out across the smooth lawn. She just couldn't take in that this wasn't her home anymore. "What about the furniture?"

"Sold along with the house," he told her. "Everything—including Pippa. I assumed that would be all right with you."

She let out a choked laugh. "It has to be, doesn't it? I'll certainly have no place to keep her while I'm gone—or when I get back, for that matter."

The old man walked over to her and put his arms

around her shoulders. "I know it hurts, dear, and I'm sorry to be the bearer of these heartbreaking tidings."

Analisa reached up and gave his craggy cheek a light kiss. "It's not your fault, Uncle Em. And don't worry about me. I'll be fine. It's just that—oh." She turned and looked all around the cozy room. "There's such a warm feeling here. A friendly feeling, as though all the people who ever lived here were happy, good people."

"You yourself have had a lot to do with that," the attorney told her. "And I honestly believe that any place you make your home will have that same warm feeling."

Her only response was a slight lifting of the corners of her mouth. How could she explain to him that she believed houses sometimes took on the personalities of their previous owners? Not just the present occupants.

She walked over to the piano and ran her fingers along the ivory keys, remembering the hours of torturous practice that had gone into making her a passable classical pianist. "When do I have to be out?"

"There's no time limit. He also said that if there's anything you want to keep but can't take to Spain with you, he'll be glad to keep it here until you get back."

She nodded. "He sounds like a nice person."

The old man grew thoughtful. "Nice isn't exactly the word I would have chosen. But I trust him. You don't meet many young men like him nowadays."

"Young?" Analisa asked, surprised. "I thought

he'd be older—I mean, if he's buying this place for someone else, he has to be reasonably well-to-do."

The old attorney could have kicked himself for letting that much slip. "Let's not worry about him, child. Just rest assured that he'll take care of the place the way it deserves, and don't worry about a thing. I'll handle all the details. Now," he changed the subject abruptly, "tell me about your date with the Spaniard last night. What did you think of him?"

She gave a little laugh. "Do you have a few hours? He's so complex, I don't know where to begin. I know he can be charming, but he doesn't seem to waste much effort on that. You can't tell what he's thinking, unless he chooses to let you know. He's cynical. And nothing seems to quite touch him . . . I just don't know."

"In other words, he's not the type of man you can wrap around your little finger like the rest of us," he chuckled. "What else?"

"His eyes. There's something there. The way they look out at the world."

The attorney nodded. "I know what you mean. He gives the appearance of finding life cheap, his own in particular. I think he's a taker of chances."

"I thought that very thing last night!"

"And what do you suppose he thinks of you?"

She delicately shrugged her shoulders. "Who can tell? I get the feeling he has tremendous resentment for me, and the awkward position he's in because of me."

"But that's not your fault!" the attorney quickly jumped to her defense.

"I know that. And I think he knows it too. But

let's face facts. Inside, deep inside, he's furious because he's cornered. If his father were in good health there would be no question of our becoming engaged. He wouldn't have anything to do with me—but as it stands, he's forced into feigning an affection he doesn't feel, agreeing to become engaged to someone he doesn't love, and all because his father can't suffer any upsets or disappointments at this point. His health is still too delicate."

"In other words," clarified the logical old man, "Santiago is being forced into living a lie and he finds it abhorrent."

"That's it in a nutshell. He's stuck with me temporarily, and it's really a pity."

"For him?"

"For both of us, I think. Whatever chance we might have had together has been ruined."

"You sound disappointed, child. Did you begin falling for him already?" He sounded almost hopeful.

"Oh, no! I didn't mean that at all! I don't even know why I put it like that. We have nothing whatsoever in common. This truce we're operating under right now is bound to be short-lived."

She had been twisting the ring he had given her last night and suddenly realized what she was doing. "Oh, and he gave me this." She held out her hand for his inspection.

The old man clicked his tongue. "Lovely. Simply lovely." His still bright eyes moved from her hand to her face. "Mind if a man who loves you gives you some advice?"

"Not at all." She smiled at him affectionately. "In fact I'd welcome it."

"All right. Here it is then. Give the man a chance. Don't shut him out because you think you know what's going on in his mind. No one ever really knows what another person is thinking—least of all a man like Rafael Santiago. Just give him a chance."

When Analisa would have questioned him as to what on earth he meant, he patted her shoulder and picked up his briefcase. "I have some other people to see while I'm out this way. Give me a call before you leave."

"Of course I will," she assured him, walking him to the door and opening it.

He kissed her on the forehead, a gesture reminiscent of Rafael's the evening before. "And you remember what I told you."

She waved as his long black car pulled out, then went thoughtfully back into the house. She'd certainly remember what he'd said—but would it ever make sense?

The rest of her day was spent in tearing the house apart, both floors, and cleaning behind, around and under everything in sight. Thoughts of Rafael interrupted her constantly, but she pushed him out of her mind and went back to work.

By the time darkness fell, she was exhausted. She soaked in a hot bubble bath and then, rather than getting dressed, even though it was only eight o'clock in the evening, slipped into a long oyster-colored nightgown with a matching robe. She brushed her hair until it fell down her back in shining golden waves, and examined it critically. If Spain was as hot as she had heard in the summer, perhaps she would be wise to get it cut. . . .

Downstairs, in the large friendly kitchen, she

poked around the cupboards and refrigerator, but discovered that she wasn't really hungry at all, so she simply made a cup of instant coffee and took it into the darkened living room. She switched on a dim light in a corner, then moved gracefully to the paino, running her fingers lightly over the ivory keys. This would probably be one of her last evenings here. Saddened by the thought, she sat down on the black-velvet-covered bench and began to play the soft, beginning strains of Brahms' Piano Concerto No. 1, the one he had written for Clara Schumann.

He had loved Clara passionately, but he had also respected and admired her husband. And both of them, in keeping with that respect, took their affair no further than their music.

On she played, unaware of the lovely picture she made sitting there with the dim light shining on her golden hair and the silken folds of her nightgown and robe, sad strains mixed with incredibly beautiful combinations. She was oblivious to her surroundings until a sound from across the room interrupted. Rafael stood there, darkly handsome, studying her with brooding eyes. There was something about him which drew her. Without thinking, she rose to her feet and began moving slowly toward him, stopping only when she was directly in front of him. Still without saying a word, he traced a long finger down her cheek. Something sparked in his eyes and his mouth moved toward hers.

Analisa closed her eyes against the shock that went through her when their lips met for the first time. She couldn't believe she was doing this, but she couldn't seem to help herself. She had been kissed before, but she had never felt quite like this. She knew she should struggle, but couldn't. She found that somehow she didn't even want to.

It was Rafael, not she, who finally pulled away and looked down at her, a mask coming down over his expression. "So, the little innocent is not so very innocent after all."

That brought her back to earth with a thump. The truce was ended. "What is that supposed to mean?"

"Exactly what you take it to mean." He moved away from her and lit a cigarette. But his eyes never left her, raking over her, making her feel vulnerable and cheap. "Do you make a habit of walking around dressed like that? Or were you expecting someone else to drop by? Perhaps I should have called first."

As his meaning sank in, she gasped. "How dare you make such insinuations!" Her green eyes flashed angrily. "And even if I were, what business would it be of yours?"

He picked up her left hand none too gently and held it in front of her. "This," he nodded toward the ring, "makes it very much my business."

"This," she retorted, "is a farce! Neither of us has any intention of marrying the other."

"What we intend to do has no bearing whatsoever on the fact that while you are wearing that ring, you will behave in a manner appropriate for my fiancée. I will tolerate nothing less."

She jerked her hand away, but her anger was cooling. "This is ridiculous. I wasn't expecting anyone anyway." No sooner were the words out of her mouth than the doorbell rang. Her heart fell. She had forgotten about John, a fellow teacher. He had told her the other day that he might drop by to borrow a book.

Rafael looked at her unsmilingly and moved past her to the door. "Go upstairs and change into something decent."

This time his voice brooked no argument. Up in her room, she threw the offending nightgown onto her bed and put on a pair of jeans and a sweater. She didn't even bother looking into a mirror before going back downstairs. He was the only man in the world who could make her so angry!

When she got to the living room, Rafael was the only one there. He looked at her arrogantly. "The young man you claim not to have been expecting has gone."

She cleared her throat in embarrassment. "I forgot he said he was coming, Rafael. I really did." She didn't know why, but she felt a need to explain it to him.

He raised a dark brow as if to say "Oh, come now."

"That does it!" she stormed. "I demand that you leave. Immediately!" she ordered, pointing to the door.

"You demand?"

"That's right." Her voice was losing some of its power under the onslaught of his assurance.

He inclined his head, and with unspeakable arrogance, sat down on one of the chairs facing the couch.

"Oh!" she gasped, outraged.

"Sit down, please."

"I most certainly will not!" she informed him, turning on her heel and starting from the room.

"You aren't going to make me come after you, are you?" he asked casually. "I would have thought you'd learned your lesson."

She stopped dead in her tracks and stood there for a moment, trying to decide what to do. Pride demanded that she finish her exit, but discretion demanded that she do as he said. Back to the couch she stalked, and sat down.

"The reason I came by was to tell you that you'll be leaving for Spain on Sunday." He tossed an airline ticket onto the coffee table between them.

She looked at it then back at him. "Sunday? I can't possibly be ready that quickly."

He raised a skeptical brow. "I understand from your attorney that the house has already been sold. What's to hold you up?"

"Well, there are . . . there are lots of things," she told him lamely, positive that there really were lots of things, but at the moment she couldn't for the life of her think of one. "Perhaps I've decided I'm not going after all," she suggested, more to provoke him than anything else.

Rafael's face didn't change expression, but there was steel in his voice. "But you haven't decided that, have you? And you won't. You will do nothing to risk my father's health. If that means we must put up with each other for however long, then we will. Is that understood?"

Analisa was ashamed of herself. "Of course. I'm sorry I said such a thing. I don't want him harmed any more than you do. Would you like some coffee, or anything?" she offered hesitantly. They had gone so quickly into open war that she didn't quite know how to handle it.

"No, thank you. I have a late flight back to Madrid, which," he looked at the gold watch on his strong wrist, "leaves in an hour and a half."

She looked at him in surprise. "You mean we're not flying back together?"

The Spaniard inclined his head. "That's correct. I have some . . . business which needs to be taken care of immediately."

That hesitation before the word "business" told her all she needed to know. He was going back because of a woman."

He rose and she followed him to the door. He looked at her downcast face and softened perceptibly. He put his finger under her chin and raised her face until she had no choice but to look into his blue eyes. "I'm sorry if I've hurt you, little witch, but as long as we have this sword hanging over our heads, even friendship is impossible between us."

She jerked her head away from him. "I don't want or need your pity, thank you."

"As you wish." His expression hardened again. "Don't forget to lock the door behind me," was his parting shot.

She watched him drive away, a frown marring her high brow. What manner of man was this Rafael Santiago? Kind and gentle one minute; arrogant and high-handed the next.

She walked back into the house, this time remembering to lock the door, turned out the one dim light that was on in the living room and went upstairs to bed. She was tired and sad. Sleep seemed the only solution.

A short distance away Rafael had pulled his car off the road and was sitting deep in thought. *"Now what,"* he breathed between clenched teeth, and pulled back onto the road.

Chapter Four

The flight to Spain seemed interminable. She alternately read, slept and fended off the would-be amorous passes of the young man sitting next to her. Her thoughts kept wandering to Rafael. She compared every man she saw or spoke to with the dark Spaniard, and they always came out on the short end. She began to think perhaps she'd been doing this ever since she was ten, and that was the reason she'd never really felt anything akin to love for another man. There was simply no one quite like him with his conflicting arrogance and gentleness.

The plane was getting ready for landing and Analisa looked out the window, examining the lush green countryside surrounding the bustling metropolis of Madrid. Spain was to be her home for the next several months, and she wanted to know everything about it she possibly could.

The plane made its final approach and as quickly as that, she was walking out onto the steaming pavement of the airfield. The dress she had on for the trip was a lovely, yellow strapless affair, held up by a band of elastic running all the way around the top. For the flight she had worn a matching jacket which she now removed. It was definitely too hot for a jacket.

Her green eyes narrowed against the glare of the sun as she walked along trying to pick out a familiar face from among the crowd of people waiting behind a fence and looking out of the building. Rafael was nowhere to be seen. Entering the building, she said a polite good-bye to the young man who had been seated next to her on the flight. He seemed disappointed that she wasn't more forthcoming, but accepted the rebuff graciously enough. She just wasn't interested in forming a lasting friendship or exchanging telephone numbers and addresses with him.

As her eyes adjusted to the darker interior of the airport, she saw him, standing in the background, dressed in a navy-blue three-piece suit. Her heart began pounding and she wondered briefly if it only beat when he was within sight.

His eyes found her at about the same time and with unhurried movements he flicked the cigarette he had been smoking into an ashtray and moved toward her.

"Hello, Analisa." His carved face was expressionless.

"Hello," she returned with a tentative smile. "I made it."

"So I see." He took her arm and they headed through the terminal. "I hope you had a pleasant flight."

"Very, thank you," she heard herself responding.

A young man who apparently recognized Rafael stopped them and began talking to him in rapid-fire Spanish, shooting appreciative glances in Analisa's direction the entire time. Rafael cut the conversation as short as he could politely do and didn't bother to introduce her to him. Insult number one, she thought resentfully as he led her outside.

"Wait a minute." She stopped dead in her tracks. "I haven't cleared customs yet, or picked up my luggage."

She flinched as he placed his hand in the small of her back and pushed her into a walking movement. "Yes you have. It has all been taken care of."

They walked to a silver Mercedes which was, predictably, in a no-parking zone. Sure enough, her luggage was being loaded into the trunk by a smiling young Spanish boy. Rafael winked at him and discreetly handed him some money. The boy's brown face beamed his thanks. Before leaving, he gave Analisa a very thorough looking over, then, to her embarrassment, gave Rafael the thumbs up sign.

The Spaniard helped her into the passenger side, but before climbing into the car himself, took off his suit coat and threw it into the back of the car, then loosened his tie and undid the top buttons of his shirt, allowing her a glimpse of strong, tanned throat. As he started the car and began moving it skillfully into the flow of traffic, she had to tear her eyes away from him before he caught her staring.

"Is it always this hot and bright here?" she asked by way of making conversation after a few silent minutes.

He looked over at her, then back at the road. "We have winter here just as you do. And now that we have covered the success of your flight and the weather, what other fascinating subjects shall we tackle?"

That hurt. She turned her face away from him so that she was looking out the passenger window.

They were moving away from the city. "Are we driving to your father's ranch?" she finally asked.

"We are going to a small airport just south of here where I have my plane, and then we will fly into Cordoba. Any other questions?" His tone was impatient.

Tears stung her eyes, and she turned her face away from him again.

"Analisa?"

Her only response was a sniff.

With a tired sigh, he pulled the car over to the side of the road and turned to her. "Analisa, look at me." His voice was softly compelling, but she couldn't bring herself to do as he asked. A firm finger under her chin brought her face around.

He took a handkerchief from his pocket and wiped her eyes, a smile twisting one side of his handsome mouth. "I think I am forever destined to wipe away your tears, little witch."

She suffered his ministrations stoically, then took the offered handkerchief when he was finished. "No, don't look away from me," he told her as she started to turn her head. "I have some things to say to you."

"Well, I for one don't want to hear them," she sniffed. "I'd just like to get this whole trip over with."

He tucked a stray strand of her golden hair behind a shell-like ear. "You hate me so much then, Analisa?" His voice was deeply soft and seductive. Her heart caught in her throat.

"Why are you doing this to me? One moment you're absolutely awful and the next you're so . . . so . . . nice," she finished lamely.

He shrugged his broad shoulders. "How can I explain this to you when I can't even to myself?" He started to say something further, but changed his mind and pulled back onto the road. The remainder of the journey to the airport was accomplished in silence.

The Mercedes pulled to a stop next to a six-seater Cessna. Rafael helped her onto the hot pavement, loaded her luggage, then helped her onto the plane.

Once strapped into their seats, she watched as he maneuvered the little aircraft every bit as skillfully as he drove a car. What next would she find out about this mysterious man? Was there anything he couldn't do?

He looked over at her, dark brow raised as the all-clear came over the radio. "Ready?"

She nodded and off they went, flashing down the runway. She watched Rafael as his strong arms seemed to lift them into the air as he handled the controls of the craft—and she knew no fear. Whatever he did, he did well.

Conversation was next to impossible with the roar of the engines, so the journey was made mostly in silence. The little plane landed in Cordoba at around eight o'clock in the evening, just as dusk was falling. Once there, he had another car waiting for him, this time a Porche. "How many cars do you have, anyway?" she asked as they got underway.

"Two. One here and one in Madrid. It makes things much simpler. And now that we can hear one another again, do you mind if I speak honestly with you about your stay in my father's house?"

She watched his profile expectantly. "No."

"Good. I allowed my father to think that the two of us hit it off rather well on my visit to your home."

"As we did, for a while," she said softly.

His blue eyes glanced over at her. "Yes. We did. And what we are going to have to do is recreate that atmosphere, repugnant as that form of playacting might be to both of us."

She nodded her head. "I understand. You don't want him upset."

"Precisely. I will have to put my arm around you occasionally, kiss you when people are looking, et cetera. I'm warning you about this so you don't flinch like you did in the airport when I touched you."

She looked over at him with wide eyes. "I did not!"

He said nothing but raised a sardonic brow in her direction.

"Well, maybe just a little," she conceded. "But I didn't mean to."

"Whether you meant to or not is unimportant. It is important that you not do it again in front of someone."

"Of course," she agreed. "I'll try not to. And you're going to have to stop baiting me."

She could feel his smile even in the darkened automobile. "Baiting you is half the fun of being with you. You always rise to it and have your say."

She smiled also and relaxed back in her seat. "Do you suppose we'll emerge from this thing friends?"

"No," he told her in no uncertain terms. "The two of us are most definitely not destined to be friends."

Analisa sighed. "That's sad, isn't it?"

"Not particularly. Spanish men seldom, if ever,

are capable of having a woman as merely a friend. Be warned."

A smile tugged at Analisa's lips as she looked out at the darkened landscape passing by. "So, tell me about the people I'll be meeting."

He thought for a second. "There's my stepbrother Manuel. He is twenty-seven, friendly, funny and nice. And from what I understand, quite a ladies' man."

"Do you like him?" she asked curiously.

There was a pause. "Yes. Yes I do. He is a likeable fellow. You will also—but watch out. If he thinks you are fair game, he'll start stalking."

"But I'm engaged to you. Doesn't that place me off-limits?"

"Not at all, at least in Spain. It only makes the chase more interesting, and the capture of the prize all the sweeter."

"I'll be careful then. Who else is there?"

"My stepsister Julia. She is your age and every bit as friendly and charming as Manuel. She is currently engaged to the ranch foreman, Jaime Francisco. You will be meeting him also as he takes his meals with the family—but he will take a little getting used to. Normally he is quite a nice fellow, but lately something has been on his mind and his charm appears to have temporarily deserted him."

"Is your sister really in love with him, or is she being forced into the marriage?"

He shrugged his broad shoulders. "Who can tell? She was once in love with him, but things change. People change."

"Yes," she agreed, "but does love?"

She felt his blue gaze on her in the darkened car.

"Not true love, no. But then how many people can claim to have experienced the real thing?"

Analisa didn't respond. She was savoring the wonderful feeling it gave her to carry on a conversation with Rafael without arguing.

"The house is at the end of this road."

She began watching more closely. They went around a bend lined with trees and straight ahead was a large, white house fashioned after the classical Spanish design. It was beautiful, and ablaze with lights. "This road we've been on for the past half an hour was the driveway, wasn't it?" she asked in awe.

"I suppose you could call it that." He pulled the car to a halt and helped her alight. They walked down a cobblestone sidewalk and up to a wrought-iron, black gate which Rafael opened noiselessly. The walk continued a short distance, with flowers abounding on either side.

He opened the enormous, heavy, carved door and they stepped into a foyer. The floor here was beautifully polished wood with an oriental rug in the center. The walls were white, and off to the sides were plants large enough to be considered trees. Beautiful oil paintings and gilt-framed mirrors lined the walls.

A middle-aged woman with graying hair pulled away from her face in a knot at the back of her head, her slender figure dressed completely in black, glided toward them and kissed Rafael on both his cheeks European style before smiling at him affectionately. "It is good to see you again so soon." She turned toward the girl on his arm and held out a surprisingly strong hand. "And you must be Analisa. Welcome to our home."

Analisa held out her own hand and thanked the woman, whom Rafael introduced in perfectly accented Spanish as his Aunt Maria.

"You speak Spanish?" she asked the girl, sounding delighted.

Analisa responded in the affirmative and continued to explain that her father had thought it an important part of her education to become fluent in at least one language other than English.

"And why did you choose Spanish?" the woman asked.

"Because I thought it was the most beautiful language I'd ever heard. I still think so, as a matter of fact."

If Tía Maria had had any doubts about this girl upon first meeting her, they were immediately laid to rest. The girl obviously had superior taste.

Rafael looked down at her with a hint of pride in his eyes. "Why didn't you tell me you spoke my language?"

"You never asked me."

Rafael raised an amused eyebrow then turned back to his aunt. "Where is everyone?"

She pointed down the hall. "In the study having some before-dinner drinks. Would you two like to freshen up before joining them?"

"I think that would be a good idea. Did you put Analisa in the rose room?"

She nodded and he turned Analisa to the right and started down the hall.

His aunt stopped him by placing a hand on his arm. "And Rafael . . . Carmen is here," she told him meaningfully.

His blue eyes remained expressionless, frustrating

Analisa's attempt to see what that name meant to him. He kissed the older woman's forehead. "Thank you for the warning, Tía."

He led Analisa down the hall, a long and wide one immediately off the one they had been standing in. The walls were covered by oil paintings and photographs which she determined to study later. He stopped in front of a large arched door and opened it for her. "This will be your room while you are here."

"Thank you." She looked up at him. "Do I have time to take a shower?"

"Of course. There's one attached to your room. I'll come back for you in, say, half an hour. Does that give you enough time?"

"More than enough." Rafael started to turn and walk away.

"Rafael?" she said tentatively.

"Ummmmmmm?" He turned back.

"Who is Carmen?"

For a moment she thought he was going to leave her without answering, but he didn't. "Carmen is a . . . friend. That's all you need to know."

She watched him walk into the room next to hers, then turned into her own. Almost magically her luggage was already there, and in the process of being unpacked by a Spanish woman who appeared to be in her forties. She very nearly gasped as she looked around the room for the first time. The walls were white and hung with paintings and mirrors. The carpeting was a deep, rich rose and the drapes and bedspread were of a lighter rose color. The woman who had been working with the luggage moved forward with a shy smile. "I'm your maid, Angela."

Analisa returned the smile. "How do you do?"

"I have already prepared a bath for you, señorita, and while you are thus occupied, I shall straighten out your clothing."

"Please, call me Analisa . . . and there's really no need for you to do my unpacking. I can take care of it later." She wasn't used to having someone do things like that for her, and it was an uncomfortable feeling.

"But that's my job!" Angela told her anxiously. "Is it that you wish another maid?"

"Oh, no. No, of course not! It's just that I've never had a maid before and I guess I don't quite know how to handle it. I'm sorry."

The tiny woman beamed at her. "Then I will teach you, no?"

"You will teach me, yes." She looked around the room again, admiring the white furniture and the way it was so beautifully carved. The bed was brass and breathtakingly large. She would have been content to look around all evening, but time, at the moment, was of the essence.

Angela helped her quickly strip out of her clothes, and this time Analisa bit back the protest that rose to her lips.

The hot bath relieved some of her travel weariness. She almost hated to get out. After toweling herself off until her skin glowed, she went through her clothes—which Angela had already neatly hung in the closet—and pulled out a sea-green dress made of a lovely gauzy material and slipped into it.

Angela brushed her hair until it shone and added a touch of lipstick. There was a knock on the door and she opened it to see Rafael, his black hair still damp from the shower. He had changed into a tan suit with a dark brown shirt unbuttoned to the middle of his strong chest. "Did I give you enough time?"

"Well, thanks a lot!" she grinned. "Obviously, even though I thought I was ready, I need some more work."

"Touché." He smiled back at her with such charm that she felt as though someone had punched her in the stomach. "I wasn't paying attention, but now that you bring it to my attention, you look beautiful, as usual."

"Honestly, we've only been engaged for twenty-three years and already you're taking me for granted!"

He looked past her at Angela and smiled. "There's no need for you to wait up for the señorita."

She gave a curtsey. "As you wish."

Analisa turned to the woman just before leaving. "And thank you for your help. I promise I'll get the hang of things soon!"

Rafael closed the door and looked down at her as they walked. "Hang of what things?"

"Luxuries—like having my own maid."

"That bothers you, having one?"

They came out of the long, paneled hallway and into the foyer where they had entered. "It doesn't bother me, precisely. It just takes a little getting used to."

They came to an elaborately carved dark-wood door. "Ready?" he asked. If she hadn't known better, she would have thought he was concerned about her.

She placed her hand over her nervous stomach and took a deep breath. "I'm sure the first time I open my mouth, the butterflies in my stomach will take flight."

Rafael threw back his head and laughed as he opened the study door and ushered her through it, his hand in the small of her back. This time she didn't flinch. She had been having such a good time talking to him that she had almost forgotten her nervousness. It now returned to her as she saw the room full of people, and she wondered if she could continue the act.

His father, Don José, whom she recognized immediately, moved toward them, still straight and tall, and clasped her hand in his while he kissed her on both cheeks in greeting. "So, you are able to make my son laugh—a rare thing, indeed." He smiled down at her. "And you are every bit as beautiful as I thought you would be."

She blushed delightfully, making the old man chuckle. "And modest as well." He turned to Rafael. "Eh, son? Your old father did well by you."

Rafael inclined his dark head.

The study was large, but friendly. The walls were paneled in the same rich, dark wood that made up the floor, and two of the walls were floor-to-ceiling bookshelves, well stocked. A huge carved leather-topped desk was in front of one of them. Another wall had a large fireplace above which hung a portrait of a beautiful woman whom Analisa knew immediately was Rafael's mother. The eyes in the portrait were as blue as her son's, and her hair just as black.

On either side of the fireplace were two long dark

leather couches, facing one another, between them a large oaken coffee table of inlaid wood sitting on an expensive-looking oriental rug.

Another wall was glass and faced a lighted courtyard with a pool. She had only a moment to absorb all this before Rafael led her forward to meet the others in the room. Rafael put his arm around her waist and led her forward to one of the couches. "This is my sister, Julia." Analisa liked her immediately. She wasn't precisely pretty, but she was certainly attractive with her dark hair and soft brown eyes. She gave Analisa a welcoming smile and held out a slender hand.

"I'm so pleased to meet you at last. We have spoken of nothing else for days now."

A smile warmed Analisa's green eyes. "Rafael has spoken of you with great affection. I hope we can become friends."

The man next to her rose and was introduced as Julia's fiancé Jaime. He shook her hand, but there was no friendliness in his gaze. She stiffened slightly in reaction and Rafael pulled her closer to his side in a protective gesture.

A handsome, dark young man next to Jaime stood also and stared at her, openmouthed. "Pull your eyes back into their sockets, Manuel. She's already taken." Rafael's voice sounded amused, but Analisa detected a hint of steel. Apparently so did his younger brother.

"Welcome, sister," he said finally, recovering and examining her up and down thoroughly but inoffensively. "I must confess my surprise. It never even occurred to me that you would be presentable, much less look like this!"

Analisa smiled at the brazen young man in spite of herself. He was handsome enough, although not in a class with Rafael. The words "not quite" came to her mind while looking at him. "Not quite" as tall as his older brother. "Not quite" as dark or as handsome, "not quite" as attractive. But it didn't seem to bother him. He had enough self-confidence for three men.

"If I were you, brother," he told Rafael without ever taking his eyes from Analisa, "I would guard her well."

Rafael raised a black brow. "I intend to, little brother." He turned to the beautiful woman on the couch next to Manuel. "And this is Señora Carmen Herrera." Analisa examined her every bit as thoroughly as the woman examined her. Thick dark hair was pulled severely away from her beautiful face, accenting high cheekbones and large black eyes. She looked to be about thirty. No wonder Rafael loved her.

The woman's dark eyes raked over the golden girl before her and hardened, although her smile never wavered. She rose gracefully from the couch and held out her hand to Analisa. "How do you do?" She then turned to Rafael and, by way of greeting, kissed him on the mouth.

Rafael's reaction was a twisted smile as he placed his hands on her shoulders and held her away from him. "I'm an engaged man now, Carmen. Perhaps such displays are best left in the past."

The woman looked at him contritely, her large eyes sad enough to melt even the hardest heart. "My apologies. I forgot myself."

Don José came up behind Analisa and touched her arm. "Come, sit next to me," he invited. "I wish to speak of your father." Her heart was heavy, which surprised her. She moved across to the couch where Tía Maria was seated next to Don José. Seating himself next to Carmen, Rafael watched her with brooding eyes.

Everyone had been speaking in English, and Don José continued in that language. "I was grieved to hear of Marcus's death. He was a great friend. A brother."

Analisa tore her eyes from Rafael and forced herself to look at her host. "He thought of you as a brother also, Don José. Some of his last thoughts were of you, and the friendship you shared."

"As mine will be of him when my time comes," he said quietly. "It has been hard on you, his death?"

"Yes. We were very close. But Rafael has helped me considerably."

Tía Maria patted her knee sympathetically. "It is good that you are here."

The old man nodded his white head. "I agree. I am only sorry that Rafael could not be with you sooner, but my health . . . ah, well, my health is not what it used to be. Old age, in some ways, is a wonderful thing. In others, not so good."

A maid walked into the study at that moment. "Dinner is served."

Don José looked at Analisa regretfully. "And I didn't even offer you a glass of sherry. What must you think of me?"

"That you're charming, as you very well know. And to tell you the truth, sir, as tired as I am at this moment, a glass of sherry would probably have put me under the table."

Don José threw back his head and laughed, causing all eyes from the opposing couch to turn in their direction. He got to his feet and offered an arm each to Analisa and his sister. She felt the curious eyes on her back as they moved into the great dining room. This was a long, thin room, with one wall composed entirely of mirrors and a table in the middle of it which could easily seat twenty people. Six chandeliers hung over it, going the length of the room. Don José moved to the head of the table and put her on his right and Rafael on his left so they faced one another, although conversation would be difficult between them.

Immediately next to Rafael was Carmen and on her left was Jaime, silently studying the American girl. Tía Maria sat regally at the foot of the table, too far away to participate in any sort of conversation. Manuel was on Analisa's right, and Julia next to him.

The food was served immediately, steaming hot. It was a Spanish dish called *paella*, and delicious. But Analisa was so tired that not only was she having a hard time following the various conversations, she could barely eat. Her host poured her a glass of sparkling white wine and shushed her when she would have protested. "Sip some of it, child, and relax. Perhaps it will give you some appetite."

Manuel grinned at her. "Lesson number one: never argue with the Santiago men. You will lose every time."

She looked at him with her golden head tilted, and

grinned back. "And lesson number two: never tell a Durant what not to do because it just makes it that much more of a challenge."

Manuel raised his wineglass to her in a silent toast. Rafael saw the gesture and frowned.

Julia touched Manuel's arm and looked across him to Analisa. "My older brother seems to want to keep you all to himself."

Analisa looked toward Rafael whose attention had once again been captured by Carmen. She watched them thoughtfully for a moment. "Didn't Rafael introduce her as Señora?" she asked both Manuel and Julia.

"Jealous?" Manuel asked.

Julia clicked her tongue at him. "She was widowed several years ago."

Analisa's eyes immediately softened with sympathy.

"Don't waste your pity," Manuel told her. "She married a man forty years her senior just to get her hands on his money, and within days of his death was chasing my brother."

Carmen placed her hand on Rafael's arm with indescribable intimacy, causing Analisa to flinch.

With dinner over, the table was cleared and coffee was served. The wine she had drunk had made her very sleepy and she tried valiantly to hide a yawn.

Rafael was apparently paying more attention to her than she thought because he rose immediately to escort her to her room. Carmen grabbed at his arm, tears in her eyes. "I will go to my grave before I will let another woman steal you from me!"

As sometimes happens in large gatherings, there

was a lull in the conversation just as she spoke the words. The muscles in Rafael's face grew taut. "You will apologize immediately!" he told the woman.

She looked up at him, her dark eyes wide. "Why should I? She has no idea what I said!"

But on the contrary, she had understood every word. For some silly reason, probably because she was tired, quick tears stung her eyes. Carmen must have been very sure of her standing in Rafael's affections to say something like that in front of his family!

Analisa rose with graceful dignity. "An apology is not necessary," she said stiffly in her perfectly accented Spanish. "And I can see myself to my room."

Rafael's blue eyes pinned her to the spot. "You will not move until she has apologized!"

Carmen was seething with resentment, but the face she showed the others was the dewy woman wronged. It would have wrung the heart of a stone. "Very well. I apologize," she said softly. "I did not realize you spoke our language." Without another word, she left the room.

Analisa turned to her host with a tired smile on her lips, even though there wasn't one in her heart. "I want very much to thank you for having me here, Don José. I'm sorry I wasn't better company."

"You are exhausted, child, and there is no need for thanks or apologies. My home is yours. You may not be the daughter of my body, but you are fast becoming the daughter of my heart. Sleep well." He rose and kissed her hand with indescribable gallantry.

Rafael moved to her side. She nodded to everyone, even the watchful Jaime. Manuel gave her a grinning thumbs up sign which she found so outrageous she nearly laughed aloud.

Julia walked over to her and took her hand lightly in her own. "Tomorrow you and I will have a long talk and get to know one another better. If you are to be my sister, I wish to know and love you as one should."

"I'd like that, Julia. Thank you so much."

Julia spontaneously kissed her cheek. "Sleep well."

She stopped by his aunt's chair. "Thank you for a lovely dinner, señora. I'm only sorry I couldn't eat more. It was delicious."

The woman's lined face softened as she gazed upon the lovely golden girl. "Please call me Tía, as everyone does." Her eyes moved to Rafael. "Now get this child to her room before she collapses in exhaustion and you have to carry her . . . unless that is what you are hoping for?" she suggested impishly.

Rafael smiled at her affectionately. "Tía, you know perfectly well that I have no need to wait until my woman faints to carry her." He effortlessly swept Analisa into his arms, taking her so by surprise that she didn't even utter a protest. "And now, if you will excuse us," he said heading for the door to the accompaniment of his father's chuckles, "I will be back . . . in a bit."

He stopped in the foyer, out of sight and ear shot of the dining room, and looked down at her. "Well, aren't you going to demand that I put you down?"

Her sleepy eyes looked into his and a slow smile curved her mouth, causing him to take a sharp breath. "Not tonight. I'm rather enjoying it." She put her head on his shoulder. "In fact, I feel I could stay this way forever."

He walked with her in his arms the rest of the way to her room. "You, my Analisa have had too much wine."

"Not at all!" she protested. "I had only one glass—to please your father."

"Then it was one glass too many for a tired girl who has eaten little or nothing all day." He switched on a light on the dresser and carried her over to the turned down bed. As he placed her on the cover, her arms tightened around his neck, her sleepy eyes focused on his carved mouth.

"Analisa, if you know what's good for you, you will let go. And stop looking at me like that."

"Like what?"

"Like you're asking for a kiss."

"And what if I am?" The words were out before she could stop them.

"Then you might get more than you bargained for."

"And if I'm willing to take a chance?"

He loosened her arms from around his neck and stood there holding them and studying her face with an enigmatic expression. He pushed the heavy strands of golden hair from her face and traced a dark circle under one of her eyes. "I'm not," he finally said, straightening. "Get some sleep and I'll see you in the morning." He took off her shoes and started for the door, but her sleepy voice stopped him.

"Rafael?"

"Yes?"

"Why do you hate me so much?"

"I don't hate you, Analisa," he said quietly.

"Then why is it so difficult for us to get along?"

"We did well enough tonight."

"But it was all an act. And it's so much work, pretending all the time. I didn't realize how much work it would be." She snuggled further down into the bed and yawned. "Are you sure you don't hate me?"

With a tired sigh, he moved back to the bed. A smile briefly touched his face when he saw that she was already nearly asleep. He leaned over and kissed her cheek. "I don't hate you, Analisa. For the first time in my life, I fear a woman."

But she didn't hear. She was already fast asleep.

Chapter Five

The next morning Analisa awoke surprisingly early, and very refreshed. She walked over to the drapes along one wall and pulled them. To her delight, two French-paned doors leading into a garden revealed themselves instead of the windows she had expected.

She very nearly skipped into the bathroom to wash her face and brush her teeth. Then she slipped into a light sundress. It was already quite warm outside. She brushed her hair into a long ponytail and stepped into the fragrant garden. There was a stone path winding through the shade-giving trees and bushes. Color was everywhere. She wished she knew more about botany so she could put a name to all the beautiful flowers surrounding her.

She left the main walk briefly and found that where the garden left off, a huge expanse of smooth green lawn took over with a white building in the distance that could easily be a stable. Once back on the main walk, she followed it as it wound back toward the house. She came out at a flagged stone veranda about three steps up and attached to the house by more French-paned doors. This was a large area with lawn furniture scattered about and even had a swingseat. A low-lying wall separated it from the main garden. A table in the middle had been set up for breakfast, but the only one there was Julia, who smiled and signaled to her to join her. "Analisa! Come have some breakfast!"

She stepped up the three stairs and sat down across the glass-topped table from the other girl. "Good morning! Isn't it beautiful here?" she asked taking a deep breath of the fragrant air.

"Yes, it is," she agreed. "You seem to have fallen under Spain's spell already."

"Oh, I have! I never dreamed . . ." She looked over at the Spanish girl and gave an embarrassed grin. "I didn't mean to go on so."

"You didn't!" Julia said reassuringly. "I, for one, find it refreshing after hearing so many complain about my country. It's a happy chance that you like it here, though, considering that it's going to be your permanent home from now on."

Analisa immediately felt guilty. She truly liked Rafael's sister and hated lying to her.

"I understand from my brother that you are a teacher?" she continued.

Analisa nodded. "I've only been doing it for a year, but I love it!"

"I don't know if Rafael mentioned it or not, but I, too, am a teacher."

Analisa's eyes lit up. "No, he didn't! Where do you teach?"

"Well, that's the thing. I don't right now, and I miss it terribly." She looked at her as though trying to decide whether or not to confide something. "I've been toying with the idea of starting a school right here on the ranch for the children of the workers."

"Don't they already have a school?"

"Well, there is one not too far away they are

supposed to attend, but the majority of the workers don't realize the value of a good education and therefore don't push their children into going—and you remember from when we were children, or at least speaking for myself, if I had had my choice between playing, or even working on the ranch, and going to school, I would never have attended classes!"

"Me neither," Analisa agreed. "But what makes you think they would attend a school on the ranch?"

A lovely young maid placed a plate before her with some croissants on it.

"Well, you see, since I know these people, I feel I could be more responsive to the needs of the children. Keep track of them better than the big public school could, give them the kind of education which would be well-rounded, but at the same time, concentrate on those subjects which will most help them as they move into the working world."

"I think that's a wonderful idea!" She took a bite of the croissant, which melted in her mouth. "Why don't you do it?"

The Spanish girl dabbed at her mouth with a napkin. "I always felt it was too big a job for just one person to tackle—at least in the beginning stages. But, now that you're here . . ."

Analisa's immediate reaction was complete enthusiasm at the idea, then it dawned on her that she would only be here for a few more months.

Julia had been watching closely. "You like it, but . . . ?"

"You're right. I like it, but . . . it's something I'll have to discuss with Rafael!" she finally said, relieved that she had thought of something.

Julia looked at her sheepishly. "I must admit to having foreseen that, and took it upon myself to mention it to him already. He thinks it's a wonderful idea."

"He does?" Analisa's voice was shocked.

She nodded her dark head happily and took a sip of the strong black coffee. "He does indeed, and has even offered his assistance in any way we might need, such as getting the proper textbooks for us in Madrid and whatever furniture we might need. There's already a building on the property which is ideal. I'll show it to you today if you wish."

"I beg your pardon?" she said distractedly. "Oh. Oh, yes, I'd like that . . . but I still want to talk to Rafael. You understand."

"Of course. When one is in love, the object of that feeling must always be consulted."

"Indeed," Analisa agreed with just a hint of sarcasm in her voice. Julia looked at her curiously, but said nothing. "And speaking of Rafael, has he breakfasted already?"

"Quite a while ago, along with Manuel and Jaime —and I believe Carmen. They are all down at the bullring right now, testing some of the bulls and heifers for courage."

Analisa nearly choked on her croissant. "Bullring?"

"Yes, of course. We breed bulls for the *corrida de toros*, so naturally we have a bullring on the property."

"Rafael never mentioned what the bulls were raised for. The thought of bullfights never even entered my mind."

Julia looked at Analisa with a cocked head, her

brow furrowed. "That seems strange considering that Rafael was once a matador." Her eyes widened at the other girl's shocked expression. "You did not know this?"

"He never said a word. . . ." Her voice was a whisper.

Julia bit her lip contritely. "Oh dear. I seem to have let the cat out of the hat!"

Analisa smiled despite her shock. "I think you mean 'cat out of the bag.'"

"Whatever. I am so sorry. Rafael will be furious. I'm sure he wanted to tell you in his own way." She gave a little smile. "But now that you know, are you not proud?"

"Proud?" she asked incredulously. "That he fights poor helpless little bulls? I don't think so."

Julia's eyes widened. "Poor, helpless little bulls? Have you ever seen an Iberian bull?"

Analisa shook her head. "No, but I've seen American bulls. They wouldn't hurt a fly!"

"I'm afraid you have quite a bit to learn, my sister-to-be. Iberian bulls are the fiercest in the world. Many matadors have been killed fighting them, and countless others badly injured. They are enormous creatures with needlesharp curving horns that can do untold damage if a person is unlucky enough to get caught on them."

Analisa swallowed hard. "And—and has Rafael ever been caught on them?"

Julia patted her hand. "All matadors have, and Rafael is no exception, but he has survived."

"I see." She felt almost sick at the thought. "And does he still fight?"

"No, at least not professionally. But he still fights

to raise funds for charities, and here on the ranch, like today. Would you like to watch? It is truly a thing of beauty, you know. Not the horror story so many have made it out to be."

Her initial reaction was indeed horror, but then a sort of terrible curiosity replaced it. "I think I would. Where will I find him?"

Julia placed her napkin on the table and pushed back her chair. "I'll take you. Have you any riding clothes with you?"

Analisa shrugged. "Just some jeans."

"That will do just fine. Let's both change, then meet back here in, say, ten minutes."

Analisa was ready first, and sat on one of the swinging seats on the veranda deep in thought. Why hadn't he told her about that part of his life? He surely must have been doing it when he and his father had visited America all those years ago, and yet no one had mentioned it to her. Perhaps Rafael had felt she didn't have the right to know—or perhaps he just cared so little for her opinion that it didn't matter to him one way or another whether or not she knew. After all, their relationship was a sham.

Julia returned with two black Cordoban hats and handed her one. "Put this on to protect you from sunstroke. It is warmer than it looks and that sun can be merciless to those unused to its strength."

She placed it on top of her head and fastened the strap under her chin. Julia eyed her with approval. "I think you are going to turn out to be one of those people who can wear anything and look stunning."

They walked down the garden path and out across the lawn to a long, slender white building which turned out to be the stable. "Rafael told me that you have your own horse in the United States."

Analisa smiled sadly. "Yes. I did. But for various reasons, she had to be sold."

Julia looked at her sympathetically. "I know how you feel. I've loved all of my horses as though they were family."

"Exactly. I was afraid I was being foolish."

"Not at all." She handed her a bridle. "Pick out whichever horse you wish, except for Diablo. He is Rafael's horse, and no one else can ride him."

"Oh, is that so?"

"Ah, I see a gleam in your eyes." She wagged a finger at the blonde girl. "I once had that very gleam—until I secretly tried to ride that black devil one day. I hit the ground so hard it was a week before I could walk without wincing!"

Analisa laughed and poked her head over the stall door with "Diablo" written on it. "He's not here."

Julia was saddling a lovely little chestnut mare. "Rafael probably rode him to the testing."

Analisa moved down the aisle looking into stall after stall. "Wait!" Julia suddenly choked. "Please, you mustn't go down there!"

Analisa looked at her curiously. "Why on earth not?"

"Please. Don't ask any questions. Just don't go any further." She walked to the other side of the stable and opened a door. There was the loveliest little blonde mare who whinnied and nuzzled Julia as she led her from the stall. "How about Babylon?"

Analisa forgot about not being allowed to look into the other stalls at the sight of the mare. She moved toward her, talking softly, cooing at her really. Babylon took an instant liking to her, and she to Babylon. She and Julia finished saddling their mounts and led the animals into the bright sunlight.

"How far away is the ring?"

Julia shrugged. "No more than two miles. Not far at all."

Rather than follow the main road which would have taken them there, they headed out across the green pastureland. Analisa reveled in the feel of the wind whipping her ponytail about, despite the hat. Both girls were superb riders and it showed in the strong way they handled their mounts. Analisa missed Pippa, but little Babylon was a good horse.

It seemed like no time at all until they were within sight of the ring. There was an enormous solid wood fence running around it, but even from a distance, on her horse, Analisa could see what was going on. It looked harmless enough. A young bull was let into the ring where there was a man on a heavily armored horse. The young bull charged the horse and hit it hard with his head, but the horse wasn't hurt because of his protective armor. Then the bull was let out of the ring.

The bullring itself was dirt, and the area surrounding it was also, which meant that there was a lot of dust hanging in the dry air. Cars were parked every which way in an area apparently designated for automobiles. Julia slowed her mount to a stop and slid off, still quite a distance from the ring. Analisa did the same, though not really understanding why. Julia took pity on her ignorance as they led their animals to an enclosed area already being used to hold other horses. "We must in no way distract the bulls' attention, you see. They might then perform badly and not be used as *corrida* bulls. One must always behave with discretion at these affairs."

Analisa was amazed at the number of people attending, and said as much to the Spanish girl. "I didn't realize this was such a big social outing."

"Oh, but it is! You see, many matadors, fine ones, come here to watch the young bulls they may someday have to fight. And the young men you see, or at least some of them, wish to prove their mettle and get in some practice with the heifers."

Julia nodded and smiled hello to many of the people as they made their way to the fenced-in area and peered in. The testing of the young bulls seemed to be halted for the moment. Analisa's eyes searched automatically for Rafael and found him smiling down at Carmen. She, of course, was lapping it up, and looked absolutely stunning in her expensive tight slacks and blouse.

Julia looked around also, then smiled. "There's Jaime. Would you mind terribly if I speak to him for a moment?"

"Of course not. I'll just stay here, if you don't mind, and watch—the goings on." That had a double meaning, but only she was aware of it.

She studiously avoided looking in Rafael's direction after that. She didn't want to see how well he got on with the Spanish woman. And she was hurt that on her first full day here he hadn't invited her to something as obviously important as this testing. A boy moved next to her. He couldn't have been more than ten, she thought. She gave him a friendly ice-breaking smile and he gave her a shy white one in return.

"My name is Analisa Durant," she finally said. "And you're . . . ?"

"I know very well who you are, señorita," he grinned, "and my name is Miguel Sanchez." He politely held out his hand, which she accepted.

"Do you come to these events often?"

"Whenever they have them. I'm going to be a great matador, you know."

"No, I didn't. Why would you want to do something like that?"

He looked at her as though she were crazy. "Because one must be courageous! Not every man can face the bulls, you know. And one can become rich just like that!" He snapped his fingers to emphasize his point. "Not to mention the women who fall at one's feet like flies!"

Analisa smiled. "Aren't you a little young to have women falling at your feet?"

"Hah! A Spaniard is never too young," he informed her.

It was a definite struggle, but she managed to refrain from smiling too broadly. "Do you live on the ranch, Miguel?"

"*Si, señorita*. My father is one of the herdsmen for the bulls."

She studied him for a long moment. "Tell me, Miguel, how old are you?"

"Twelve," he informed her proudly.

"Shouldn't you be in school, then?"

"Are you kidding?" he scoffed. "What need have I for schooling? I am to be a great matador!"

"Well, even matadors have to count their money and write love letters, don't you think?"

"I shall pay someone else to do it," he informed

her grandly. "Sshhh. The part with the heifers is about to begin and Don Rafael is always first."

As she watched, Rafael entered the ring and all six feet plus of him stood there quietly, his eyes unwaveringly on the chute near where she was standing. He looked so handsome in his short-jacketed black suit and Cordoban hat that her heart began pounding furiously. She took some deep calming breaths. "How dare he be so attractive!" she thought irrationally.

"Tell me something, Miguel. Why isn't he on horseback like the other man I saw as I rode up?"

"He was testing the young bulls for their courage, to find out whether or not they are worthy of being raised to fight in a *corrida*. All bulls are tested when they are about two, but always on horseback, never on foot with a cape. Bulls have very long memories. Once they have fought a man with a cape, they never forget."

"You mean they come to realize that the man is the enemy and not the cape?"

He actually seemed proud of her. "Exactly! And they will then charge the man."

She shivered as a loud noise from the ring caught her attention.

She didn't know what she had been expecting, but it certainly wasn't the enormous animal which burst from the chute. The thick lump of muscle on its neck was raised, its black flanks heaving as it toured the ring with hot eyes. Then it spotted the lone man.

Without any warning whatsoever, it charged, fast and furiously. She wanted to scream but the sound caught in her throat. Rafael was going to die and all she could do was watch in horror. Then, for the first time, and all in the matter of a split second, she noticed that he had a magenta and yellow cape in his hand.

With his body absolutely stationary, he flicked the cape with his wrists and the creature whooshed by him, the lethal needlesharp horns stabbing harmlessly into the cloth, only inches away from his body. The only thing that touched the man was the dirt churned by the pounding hooves.

She couldn't take her eyes off the ring, but her voice was full of unadulterated fear. "Miguel, I thought you said that was a heifer!"

"It is," he confirmed. "What, did you think that because it is a female its horns would be shorter, its wish to kill less?"

"Something like that," she said weakly.

He shook his black mop of hair. "They are just as vicious and dangerous as bulls. Sometimes more so!"

Her eyes never left the heifer, whose eyes never left the man. "But I don't understand. What's the point of this? Is it just for . . . fun?"

"Boy, you really don't know anything about bull-fighting, do you?"

"Well, no!" she said defensively. "It's not exactly the number one sport in America, you know."

The boy clicked his tongue. "You see, señorita," he explained as though talking to a rather backward child, "in order to produce brave bulls, it is necessary for them to have brave mothers. For this they must be tested, and if they are courageous enough, they are mated with one of the brave bulls who is not being sent to the *corrida*. And after this we will be testing some of the young bulls which will be kept on the ranch for breeding purposes. They must prove courageous also, you know, or they won't produce good offspring. But there is some risk. Once they have been caped, they may not be sold as *corrida* bulls. It is against the law."

During this explanation her eyes hadn't left the ring. The heifer charged again, this time coming so close to Rafael that the right horn ripped his jacket. There was no blood, but Analisa thought she would surely faint. And she probably would have, but the animal skidded to a halt, wheeled about more quickly than she would have believed possible and charged again. Rafael just stood there, motionless, waiting. At the last second, when the bull was a yard from him, he gave the cape a gentle flick and the animal veered off its course, following the lure, and thundered harmlessly past him.

Rafael then turned his back on the animal, his cape over his arm, and casually walked from the ring, not once looking back to see if it had decided to charge again.

Analisa, hand at her throat, turned around, her back against the solid fence, and slid into a sitting position. Her knees had had about all they could take. Miguel clicked his tongue sympathetically. "Poor Yanqui. You know, though, Señorita Durant, that if you are to be his wife, this is something you must get used to."

She wrinkled her nose expressively and the boy laughed. "You will watch the next exhibition, no?"

"Oh, I really don't think so, Miguel. My heart has already taken quite a punishment for one day."

"Please? I would be honored if you would do so."

She couldn't imagine why the next one would

mean so much to him, but she nodded her golden head. "All right. I'll watch."

"Gracias!" he grinned. "And now I must go." He bobbed her a hurried little bow and raced off, darting gracefully between the people. She smiled to herself as she watched him. He was a prime example of what Julia had been talking about earlier. A warm, intelligent child who was receiving no encouragement to go to school. Miguel could do wonderful things with his life if only he had someone to guide him over the rough spots. And how she herself would delight in helping him!

A shadow fell over her. "What are you doing here?" Rafael's voice demanded angrily from somewhere above. Her eyes located his boots then traveled up over his well-muscled thighs, flat stomach, broad chest and finally found his blazing blue eyes. She wrinkled her nose and squinted into the bright sun. "Julia brought me with her. Why?"

"If I had wanted you here, I would have invited you."

Those were most definitely fighting words, but it was rather difficult to strike back while sitting ignominiously on the ground. She stood up, without his assistance, and brushed the dust off her jeans.

"Well, since you couldn't be troubled to mention it to me one way or the other, there was no way I could have known that, is there?"

"Did it perhaps occur to you that I knew you well enough to know that had I mentioned it to you, you would have come whether I wanted you to or not?"

She pretended not to have heard that. "While we're on the subject, *Don Rafael,* the least *you* could have done was told me you were a matador. Your sister informed me of it today and I'm sure she thinks I'm the most peculiar fiancée in the world not to know what her husband-to-be does for a living!"

"*Did* for a living," he corrected. "Now I am an architect."

"Oh, well excuse me! That, of course, makes it all right that you didn't tell me!"

A group of men dressed in clothes similar to those of Rafael's interrupted at that moment and began discussing some of the bulls they had seen that day, their good points and bad. Rafael talked with them for a good ten minutes while some of them leered unobtrusively at Analisa. He never bothered to introduce her to them. She most definitely felt put in her place, once again. When they finally moved away, he turned back to her, concern having replaced the anger in his blue eyes. "I was going to tell you, in my own way, in my own time. You must believe me when I say that I didn't want you to find out from someone else. North Americans have no understanding of this." He gestured toward the *corrida*.

"Well *this* North American certainly lives up to your low expectations. What on earth is the point of what you did out there just now? You could have gotten yourself killed, or at least badly injured, and for what? It's crazy!"

He raised a sardonic black brow. "Ah, but then you would have been free from your obligation. I should have thought you'd be cheering for the animal."

Analisa stamped her foot in frustration. "Honestly! There's just no talking to some men!"

He smiled, but said nothing, his gaze moving to

the *corrida*. His expression was serious suddenly and Analisa turned to see what he was looking at. Little Miguel had entered the ring, cape in hand, and was standing there looking at a chute.

She grabbed Rafael's arm. "You have to get him out of there!"

"No," he said succinctly. "He wishes to be a matador and this is the only way he will ever learn his trade."

"But he could be killed!"

Rafael shrugged. "Knocked around a bit, perhaps, but not killed. The animal we have chosen for him is small."

"But Miguel is just a baby." She tried futilely to change his mind.

"Don't let him hear you say that," he advised. "His offense would know no bounds."

A small bull came charging out of the chute. To little Miguel, standing there so bravely, the animal must have appeared huge. It pawed the ground a bit as a threat before actually charging. Miguel looked as though he would have loved to take flight but he stood still, moving the cape in much the same way Rafael had, but with less assurance.

Analisa's breath came out in a relieved gasp as the animal rushed by without touching the boy. Again and again the small animal rushed past, charging the cape, and Miguel visibly gained confidence. Perhaps too much confidence, because he flicked his wrist improperly on one of the passes and the animal crashed into his small form.

Before she could even scream, Rafael was over the fence and in the ring, coaxing the animal to run at him instead of charging the inert form of the boy.

The calf charged right into the open chute behind him and the heavy gate clanged shut on it. The Spaniard sprinted over to the boy, who was now sitting up and patting his abdomen, the point of impact. Other men had by this time jumped into the ring also and gathered around the small form. Rafael appeared to ask him a few serious questions, then helped him to his feet. He stood there shakily for a moment, then still slightly bent, walked unaided from the ring to the cheers of the onlookers.

Analisa raced around the dusty *corrida* to the gate he was coming through, dodging all the people, ready to take him into her arms the moment she saw his pale little face emerge, but Rafael grabbed her arm in an iron grip. "No! Leave him his pride. All young men must take their knocks if they wish to become matadors. Perhaps the lesson he learned today will keep him from getting killed another day."

Analisa shook her head in amazement. "How can you be so callous about this? He could be seriously hurt!"

Rafael placed both hands on her slender shoulders and turned her toward him, away from the boy who was now seated several yards away. "Analisa," he sighed. "Will you accept that you know nothing about this and keep out of it? I know what I'm talking about. Coddling him now would only cause him embarrassment. You wouldn't want to do that, would you?"

"Well, no, but . . ."

"There are no buts here, woman." A corner of his shapely mouth lifted. "Would you like to stamp your foot again and get it out of your system?"

Her own mouth lifted at the corners. "As a matter of fact, I'd love to, but I'll resist."

"Good girl." He leaned over and surprised her by lightly kissing her forehead. "Now, if you will excuse me, I'd like to have a talk with the boy."

Her smile of amusement changed to one of wonder at the many moods of the man. Her eyes followed him, reluctant to move away, until she saw Carmen glaring at her. Then the smile slowly faded. It served as a reminder that Carmen was the woman he loved. Her happiness of a moment before left her and in its wake was emptiness. What was happening to her?

A hand came down on her shoulder in friendly fashion, causing her to jump with the unexpectedness of it. "Hello, little sister to be. Why so sad looking all of a sudden?"

She looked up at Manuel and shrugged her delicate shoulders. "Perhaps I'm just a sad person."

He shook his dark head. "I don't think so. Are you just realizing what it's like to be in love with a matador?"

She looked back at Rafael, now deep in discussion with little Miguel, apparently telling him where he had gone wrong. "Perhaps that's it," she said softly. "But then no one ever said it would be easy! Shall we change the subject?"

Manuel's brown eyes studied her for a moment, then he nodded. "As you wish. What would you like to discuss? The weather, perhaps? It certainly is a warm one today, is it not?"

Analisa broke into a smile, taking Manuel aback with its innate charm. "Yes, indeed, sir, it is quite warm. I wonder what tomorrow will bring?"

Carmen walked, or strutted, over to them, her black eyes flashing. "So, one man isn't enough for you? You have to have everyone in sight! Rafael won't stand for it, you know!"

"Down, Carmen," advised Manuel. "Your claws are showing."

"I don't care!" Her gaze raked over the other girl, looking at her long golden hair as though she would have enjoyed pulling it all out, strand by strand. "She thinks she can come here and dig her hooks into *my* Rafael, but she can't. I will see to it. It's me he loves!"

Analisa felt as though she had taken a hard punch to the stomach. Of course it was Carmen he loved, but to hear it said aloud . . . well, that was something else again.

Manuel was getting angry and was about to retort, but Analisa placed a restraining hand on his arm. "Please. Let her have her say. It's best to have everything in the open." Manuel clenched his jaw but said nothing.

Carmen's eyes narrowed. "You think you are so clever. Well, we'll just see how clever you are at keeping my Rafael when he realizes just what he's gotten himself into! A squeamish little Norte Americana who can't stand the sight of a bullfight, unless I miss my guess! How long do you think he'll put up with that? In no time he'll realize his infatuation with you for what it is and come back to me, have no doubt."

Analisa's green eyes widened. Infatuation? With her? Then she didn't know about the arrangement! He hadn't told her that they had no intention of marrying!

"That's enough!" Julia had arrived and was glaring at Carmen. "You will say nothing more, for if you do, I will tell it all to Rafael and he will see you as you truly are!"

Carmen looked at the other Spanish girl in astonishment. "You would take her side against me?"

"She is to be my sister. Yes, I take her side."

Carmen looked at all three faces, then turned and walked away without another word. Julia looked at Analisa apologetically. "I must apologize for Carmen. I hope she has not caused you too much grief?"

"She was horrible," Manuel blurted out, "and I for one don't think Analisa should be left alone with her. There's no telling how far she'll go in her blind rage to win Rafael back."

Analisa hooked her arms through theirs. "I would probably feel the same way in her place. And for heaven's sake, don't you two start worrying about me. I'm not nearly as helpless as I apparently appear."

Julia patted her hand. "Have you had enough of this for your first day?"

"I think so. It's all rather heartstopping, isn't it?"

"Indeed. Would you like to ride to the proposed schoolhouse, then? I'm sure Rafael wouldn't mind if we left."

"What wouldn't Rafael mind?" he asked, walking over to them.

Julia smiled up at him affectionately. "If I took Analisa to view the building we have in mind for the schoolhouse."

"Ah, yes. The schoolhouse." He looked down at Analisa. "I see you two have already discussed that."

"That's right," his betrothed confirmed. "And I must say I'm surprised to hear that you favor such a thing."

"I rather thought you would be." He turned to his sister. "I think riding out there is a wonderful idea. I'm sorry I won't be able to join you. How about you, Manuel?"

He shrugged his shoulders. "I've seen enough of these tests. Riding out with you ladies will be a welcome break."

"Good." Then he turned to Analisa. "I had hoped to take you on a picnic today, but it looks as though these tests will be going on into the late afternoon. Perhaps you'd like to go tomorrow. There's something I'd like you to see."

"I'd love it!" She couldn't think of a thing she'd rather do than go on a picnic with Rafael.

"And you two as well," he smiled at his brother and sister. "I haven't forgotten all the rules yet."

"Rules?" Analisa looked at all of them in turn. "What are you talking about?"

"In Spain," Julia explained, "although some families have taken on western ways regarding courtship, here we look askance at couples, unmarried couples, taking off on their own for any length of time without being properly chaperoned. It is felt to bring dishonor upon the woman to be alone in the company of a man."

Analisa looked at her in disbelief and Julia crossed her heart in the international sign of veracity. "Truly. Here in Andalusia it is most important not to offend sensibilities."

Rafael smiled down at the two girls and winked at his brother. "I'll let the two of you explain the finer points of Cordoban and Andalusian life to my betrothed. I have some things to take care of."

He started to walk away, then turned back, raised Analisa's face to his and kissed her lightly on the mouth. "Public displays of affection are also frowned upon here," he informed her wickedly as he walked off.

She watched him until he was out of sight. Sometimes it was difficult for her to remember that any kindness he showed her was strictly for public consumption. She turned to her two companions with a heartfelt sigh. "Well, shall we?"

Chapter Six

The three young people collected their horses and rode over the pastures once again, this time in a different direction. Analisa kept looking for bulls—after all, they grazed in these pastures, or so she believed, but she never saw any.

Manuel seemed to know what she was looking for. "You're right, you know. They are out there somewhere, but chances are you won't see them. And even if you do, there is nothing to worry about."

Analisa looked at him in disbelief. "How can you say that, after what I just witnessed?"

"The bulls run in herds," Julia explained. "And as long as they are with other bulls, or oxen, they won't attack. It's if they get separated from the herd that they become dangerous and attack anything that moves."

"For some reason, that's not very comforting."

Manuel gave her an encouraging smile. "Seriously, don't worry. I've been riding through these pastures since I was just a boy, and have never been attacked yet."

The horses picked their way across the pasture to a paved one-lane road. This they followed around a tree-lined bend, and off to one side was a small adobe building.

"This is it," Julia told her. "It used to be a home, but the old couple who lived here passed on years ago."

The three dismounted and tied their mounts to some shrubbery outside the building. Julia and Manuel went inside, but Analisa studied the outside for a moment. Vines were climbing up the adobe, some of them green, some dead and brown and scraggly. The grass surrounding it was sparse, and there was an equal amount of dirt and grass showing. And what grass there was was overgrown. The few hedges, however, were surprisingly healthy.

She walked inside and had to stand still for a moment while her eyes adjusted to the dim interior. "Don't let the lack of light put you off," Julia told her. "Rafael is going to have some workers knock out part of the wall on the shady side and install windows."

"That will certainly cheer it up a bit. But what about the location? Is it central enough for the children to reach easily?"

"Absolutely. There should be no problem with that at all," Julia assured her.

Manuel inspected the room, poking into all four corners. "Can you imagine living your life in a one-room house?"

Julia shook her head. "Not really, but I understand the old couple lived here quite happily for nearly fifty years."

Analisa blew some dust off a table in the middle of the room—the only furniture there—and looked around. "I think the place has potential. It's big enough in here to have two classes going on at once. We could have half the desks facing one way, the other half the other way. That might help separate the really young students from the older ones."

"Already we are thinking alike," Julia smiled.

"But"—she hesitated—"what if something happened to one of us—such as, say, starting a family. Would only one teacher be able to run it?" That, Analisa knew, was the most important question of all. After all, she wasn't going to be here in another three months or so, and Julia would be left holding the bag.

"I don't think that will be a problem at all," Julia said. "The first few weeks of operation will be the roughest. After all, we will have all age groups here to instruct, which means more preparation time than normal, but once the children get the hang of us, and we of them, things should run smoothly, even with just one of us—and even if one of us does start a family, we can always get outside help."

"Well, personally," Manuel threw in, "I think your biggest job is going to be getting this place cleaned up enough to use."

Both girls' eyes zoomed in on him. He looked from one to the other and hastily backed out of the little house and into the sunlight. "Oh no you don't," he told them as they followed him out. "You want to use this old place for a school, you can clean it up yourselves!"

He grabbed the reins of his horse and leaped on its back before the girls could catch him. "I suddenly have remembered an important engagement. See you later!" He galloped off at full tilt.

The girls turned to each other and burst into laughter. "I didn't say anything. Did you say anything?" Julia asked between gasps.

"Not a word!" Still laughing they went back into the house where their happiness ended on a sigh of hard work to come. "I suppose we could get some done this afternoon if you happen to have some cleaning materials with you."

Julia pointed to a darkened corner of the room. "As luck would have it I brought some things out yesterday."

A little over two hours later they had washed down one of the walls and swept the floor clean preparatory to scrubbing it.

It was a hot afternoon and both girls were drenched with perspiration and covered with dust. Julia looked over the finished wall and turned to Analisa. "I don't know about you, but the only thing I want to do at this moment is take a long, leisurely swim in the pool. How about you?"

"That sounds lovely—but there are two things holding me back. The first is that I don't know how to swim, and the second is that I didn't bring a bathing suit with me."

"The second is no problem. We keep extras in the guesthouse. But the first—I must say I'm surprised. I thought all American girls knew how to swim."

"Well not this one, I'm sorry to say. And now I'm probably too old to learn. What do you think?"

"Do not be ridiculous. Rafael will teach you in no time. He is an excellent swimmer."

Analisa smiled. "Somehow I thought he would be."

"That's some brother I have, don't you think?" Julia asked proudly.

"Yes, I do think." Analisa smiled sadly. "I rather imagine once a woman has been in love with Rafael she's ruined for any other man."

Julia looked at her sharply. "Are you referring to Carmen?"

Analisa was startled. Carmen? Of course she was talking about Carmen. Who else? Who else, indeed. "I know just how I'd feel in her place."

Julia looked at her with a serious expression. "Let me give you some sound advice. Do not be blinded by pity for her. She will show you no mercy in trying to come between the two of you, and I suggest you keep your guard up at all times with her. Unfortunately her late husband was a great friend of our father's or else we could show her the back door."

"But Rafael has a great affection for her."

"I disagree. I think he feels sorry for her. And he has only seen Carmen on her best behavior. And . . . she is a beautiful woman. Do not all men love beautiful women?"

Analisa shrugged. "I suppose—but I think their relationship goes a bit deeper than that."

"An affair you mean?"

Analisa flinched from the bald terminology. "Yes."

"Perhaps. Perhaps not. You can be certain Carmen would have made herself available. But an affair of the heart? Who can tell with Rafael? He has never worn his heart on his sleeve—as opposed to Manuel, who hangs it there for all to see. The only time I have known him to talk about anything like this at all was when, over the years, he has rebelled against an arranged marriage."

"With me."

"With anyone. That's how I know the two of you are not really planning to marry."

Analisa's startled green eyes met knowing brown ones. "You know?"

"I guessed initially. Now I know." She smiled at her reassuringly. "Don't worry. I won't say anything. I know you are both doing it for father."

Analisa sat down on the floor with a sigh and Julia joined her. "It's a relief not to have to lie to you anymore. I just hated that."

Julia nodded. "May I ask you something? Are you in love with my brother?"

"Of course not!" Analisa denied quickly. A little too quickly to Julia's way of thinking. "This arrangement has been foisted upon me as well."

"Good. You see, over the years Rafael has become used to having any woman he wanted, on his terms. It is one of the phenomenons of bullfighting. Women can't resist the matador. Particularly one who looks as Rafael does. He takes women for granted because they have always been there for him. For you, falling in love with my brother would mean certain hurt."

"Oh." Analisa was thoughtful for a moment, remembering a conversation she had had with Rafael. "You know, he told me once that there had been a girl whom he loved. Above all others, apparently. Do you know anything about her? Did she die?"

Julia's brow creased in thought, but she finally shook her head. "I'm afraid I can't help you—unless it has something to do with a terrible argument he and father had years ago. I couldn't have been more than ten, but I remember it so very clearly. And it was about a woman. Rafael left after that and only came back infrequently. Not like he used to."

So, Analisa thought. There had been someone in his life whom he had loved. Perhaps he would never love again. What she couldn't understand, though, was why, unless the girl was dead, or married to someone else, he hadn't married her against his father's wishes. He seemed the kind of man who would take what he wanted, when he wanted it. Period.

Julia leaned over and kissed Analisa's cheek. "I wish we really were going to be sisters, you and I."

Analisa smiled at her softly. "I do also. Thank you. Of course, there's always Manuel," she suggested impishly.

"Perish the thought," laughed Julia. "Manuel may be gay and charming, always ready with the comeback, but he is still a little boy, and I think he always will be. He lives on his charm. He has to. He was too lazy to finish college, or to hold a steady job. You know," she said thoughtfully, "I've always tried to avoid comparing my two brothers, but one thing stands out in my mind. Rafael, I feel sure, has been with many women, but when, or perhaps I should say if, he ever finds the right one, if he ever falls in love, that will be it for him. No more mistresses or lovers. Manuel on the other hand, seems to be rather shallow when it comes to his feelings for women. They are there for his pleasure today, gone tomorrow. Whomever he marries will have to put up with endless affairs and heartache."

She got to her feet and dusted down her jeans. Analisa did likewise. "Well, on that note, shall we head back for the house? Rafael should be finished with the testing by now."

They arrived back at the house a little over an hour later. Even from the foyer it was evident that Manuel, Rafael and Carmen were already in the pool—and having a wonderful time. Julia smiled at her. "Don't go getting all insecure again. We will have you swimming like a fish in no time. And now, you go to your room while I get you a suit from the guesthouse." The Spanish girl walked through the living room and the sliding glass doors to the large pool and called a greeting to the others. Analisa heard Manuel ask where she was—not Rafael, mind you, but Manuel. With a sigh, she headed down the hall to her room. Angela was already there.

"I saw you coming," she smiled. "What is your pleasure? Bath or shower? And what would you like to wear afterward?"

Analisa smiled at the middle-aged woman. "Shower, please, and Julia is going to be dropping off a bathing suit."

Angela bustled into the powder room and got the water running while Analisa took off her dusty clothes. She took a long, leisurely shower and thought over what Julia had said to her. The thought of Rafael loving someone was like a great weight on her chest. It disturbed her more than she was willing to admit.

Angela wasn't in the room when she got out of the shower, but a black bathing suit was laid out on the rose-colored bed. Black was a good color on her. She held it in her hand and looked at it curiously. It

89

was one piece, but there still didn't appear to be much of it. She put it on and looked into a mirror. Her emerald eyes grew wide. Talk about a sexy bathing suit! Her long legs were bare nearly to the hipbone. The material in the front of the suit tied behind her neck, but took a dive between her breasts which was certainly eye catching. She knew from having seen fashion pictures in the States that this was what was being worn nowadays, but somehow looking at it on someone else was quite different from wearing it oneself.

She went through her closet and came up with a short, white terrycloth jacket which she used as a robe with her shorty nightgowns. It looked indistinguishable from a beach jacket and she slipped into it and examined herself in the mirror again. Much, much better. Her long legs were still very much in evidence, but that was about all.

She went to the pool the way she had seen Julia do, through the living room, and smiled at the sight that met her eyes. Manuel and Julia were trying to dunk each other and were laughing and splashing madly. Carmen pulled herself out of the cool blue water, climbed the high divingboard and jackknifed beautifully into the water. Julia climbed out onto the edge of the pool calling encouragement to Manuel, who had taken off after Carmen for some more dunking.

Rafael came up behind her, a towel thrown around his neck. Apparently he had just arrived also. She looked up at him. "I thought you were already out here?"

"That would be a little difficult. I just got back."

"How did it go?" What she really wanted to know was whether or not anyone had gotten hurt.

He surprised her by giving her a devastatingly slow smile, showing strong white teeth. "Miguel is just fine, and no one else was injured."

"How did you know what I was thinking?"

He reached out a strong finger and touched her face. "You are one of the most transparent women I've ever met."

Her breath caught in her throat at his touch. She could only hope that what his touch did to her wasn't registered on her "transparent" face.

Julia saw them and waved for them to join her. They walked over the smooth wet cement and sat next to her, Analisa in the middle. "I hope the suit fits you all right." The Spanish girl's eyes were twinkling.

"You know exactly how the suit fits," Analisa told her with a slight shake of the head.

"Is that the reason for the jacket?"

"Well I had to put something over it!"

"What are you two talking about?" Rafael asked.

"The bathing suit your sister found for me," Analisa told him, "or lack thereof."

Julia just laughed and dove cleanly into the pool. Rafael looked her over speculatively. "That jacket makes it difficult to see what you are talking about."

"I know." She didn't elaborate.

"Rafael! Help!" Carmen called from the middle of the pool. Julia and Manuel had ganged up on her and were laughingly trying to dunk her.

"Ah, a damsel in distress." He sounded vaguely annoyed, but rose and gave Analisa a bow. "If you will excuse me for a moment, I must slay the dragons." He swam strongly out to where the action was while she watched. She didn't really see anyone but Rafael. His swimming trunks were navy blue and brief, and his muscular body was bronzed all over, as far as she could see. His chest had just the right amount of black, curly hair on it. When he swam, the muscles in his shoulders rippled with the movement. Even his stomach was muscular. Watching him, Analisa was reminded of a Michelangelo sculpture.

When Carmen had been rescued, he swam back to her and rested his arms intimately on her legs while he looked up at her. Her heart was thumping. "Are you just going to sit there and look wistful, or are you going to join us?"

"She's going to join us!" Manuel yelled, picking her up bodily and running with her to the deep end and unceremoniously throwing her in before she could tell him that she couldn't swim.

She frantically fought her way to the top, taking in great gulps of water along the way. Just as she surfaced, chokingly, something tugged at her leg before she could get any air, and under she went again.

She was beginning to feel faint from lack of air as she fought her way up again. She heard Julia yell that she couldn't swim and suddenly, wonderfully, strong arms went around her and held her up as they pulled her through the water to the edge. Rafael lifted her out of the water onto the edge of the pool, then climbed out next to her, taking her into his arms as she coughed the chlorinated water out of her system.

When she finished, he held her away from him and

pushed her wet hair off her forehead. "Are you all right now?"

She nodded. Her throat felt as though it was on fire.

"Perhaps, Manuel," he said with tightly controlled anger, "you would do well to ask if the person you are about to throw in can swim."

"It's not his fault," Analisa defended hoarsely. "I should have said something as soon as I came out. I mean, how many people do you know who can't swim in this day and age?"

Manuel knelt next to her also and lightly touched her hair. "That is no excuse. Rafael is right to be angry."

"Are you sure you are all right?" Julia asked worriedly.

"Oh, for heaven's sake," Carmen said disgustedly from the pool. "What's all the fuss about? She took in a little water, which we all do from time to time. She's perfectly fine."

Analisa felt terrible. She had certainly put a pall on what had started out to be a fun afternoon. She moved away from Rafael and sat up straight. "Carmen is absolutely right. I feel like a complete idiot. And the best way for me to overcome any fear of swimming I might have is to learn to do it properly. Any volunteers?"

Rafael looked at her with a hint of pride in his eyes and slid into the water. They were at the shallow end. He raised his hands to her waist and lowered her gently next to him. "Do you know how to float?"

"I don't know. I've never tried it."

"Well, the first thing you're going to do is take that silly jacket off," Julia informed her, taking it away with her. Rafael looked her up and down, then raised an expressive dark eyebrow.

"Why you would want to cover up a figure like that, I can't imagine." Analisa could feel the color flood her cheeks. Rafael smiled at her gently. "Analisa, you're a beautiful woman. Don't try to hide it."

She let out an exasperated breath. "Are you going to teach me to swim or not?"

He led her further from the edge. "Lean back," he instructed. "Let your back touch the water and then raise your legs until you can see your toes." She did as she was told, the hand he placed in the middle of her back giving her confidence. "Good girl. That's it. Get your hair wet."

He began moving her through the water, staying close to her. Then he removed his hand. At first she panicked, but his voice was deeply soothing as he gave her encouragement and soon she was floating on her back as though she'd done it all her life. Then he turned her over on her stomach, and soon he had her holding onto the edge of the pool and kicking her legs. Both Manuel and Julia stayed near giving her pointers where they thought useful, and encouraging her when she needed it.

Carmen got disgusted with the whole thing and went into the house.

"That about does it," Rafael said after about forty minutes of instruction. "I think that's enough for one lesson. We'll practice some more tomorrow. If I can't be here, I'm sure Manuel will help you."

"No problem," Manuel agreed. "I would be happy to."

Rafael lifted her out of the pool and onto the edge. "Now, if you will excuse me, I want to do a few laps before dinner." Analisa watched admiringly as he stroked his way cleanly and strongly through the blue water. Manuel and Julia both got out of the pool and sat next to her.

"I told you he would teach you to swim," Julia said.

"I still can't believe you didn't know how," Manuel told her, looking her up and down. "You look as though you were born to wear a bathing suit."

Julia looked at him significantly. "Watch it brother."

Analisa rose to her feet and wrapped a towel around herself. "If you two don't mind, I think I'm going to lie down a bit before it's time to eat."

"Dinner is at nine o'clock. We will see you then," Julia offered.

Back in her room, she took off the wet bathing suit, wrapped herself in a robe and was asleep within moments of her head touching the pillow.

Chapter Seven

When Angela awakened her two hours later, she was astonished that she had slept so long. Before coming to Spain, she never took naps unless she was ill. She dressed for dinner in a pale yellow cotton dress which had a peasant-style top and flared skirt. Angela brushed out her long blonde hair until it shone and pinned a white rose over her left ear.

"I was told to tell you that cocktails will be taken on the veranda this evening," the Spanish woman told her. "Don José enjoys the out-of-doors."

"I do too," Analisa smiled. "Especially here. And the garden fills the veranda with such heady perfume."

"Señora Santiago—Rafael's mother—had the veranda built for just that reason. And that is why there is so much furniture out there, so many people can enjoy it. You will probably be having dinner outside rather than in the dining room also."

Analisa got a faraway look in her eyes. "You know, my father and I always enjoyed having dinner in our back yard when the weather permitted. Naturally our patio had nothing of the elegance of the veranda here, but we always had fun."

Angela looked at her sympathetically. "You still miss your father, señorita?"

Analisa nodded. "Particularly now. There are so many things I'd like to talk over with him. My father had an uncanny ability to take something terribly confusing, and with one sentence, turn it into something easily understandable."

"And you have a need for that now?"

She gave a little laugh. "Most definitely."

"Perhaps Don José could be of some help to you. He is a wonderful, kind man who loves nothing better than to take someone else's troubles and make them his own."

"I know. But I'm afraid this isn't something he'll be able to help me with. I'll just have to find the answers on my own."

"What about Don Rafael? Can he not help you find the answers you search for?"

Analisa rose to her feet and started out the door into the garden. "He, Angela, is the question. . . . There's no need for you to wait up for me."

"As you wish. I will see you in the morning then."

Analisa took her time walking down the charming path. It wasn't quite dark out yet, but there was that certain glow in the sky that comes with the setting sun. She inhaled the perfumed air deeply, touching a blossom here and there, stopping occasionally to listen to the coming night noises.

Along the walk she occasionally came across small alcoves with long, wrought-iron benches made secluded by the tree branches overhanging them. She sat on one very quietly before joining the others. At some point in time, she had a lot of thinking to do, and this was a lovely place in which to start.

"What do you mean you've changed your mind?" Carmen's voice carried across the garden to her, catching her attention. "You know as well as I that if she has her way and marries Rafael, your little jig is up, as they say."

The voice was coming from the alcove hidden directly behind the one Analisa was in. She had no wish to eavesdrop and started to make her presence known, but stopped when she heard Jaime's voice.

"Then that is the way it goes. She has done me no harm and I will not do any to her."

"You are nothing but a coward. Do you not care that if Rafael marries her everything that would have gone to Julia will now go to him and that Americana?"

"Lack of courage has nothing to do with this, and you know it."

"I know no such thing. You got engaged to that mousy Julia because of her prospective inheritance. What are you going to do now?"

"Go through with the marriage."

"Don't tell me you have fallen in love with her!"

"I owe you no explanation—but the fact of the matter is that I have. If she comes to me with her inheritance, or if she comes to me with nothing but the clothes on her back, it matters not." Analisa gave Jaime a silent thumbs up sign from her seat in the hidden alcove.

"Never did I think I would hear such drivel fall from your lips."

"Is that all you wanted, Carmen?" he asked

impatiently. "I would like to get back to the veranda."

"No, that's not all. You agreed to help me get rid of Rafael's betrothed, and the time is right."

"I agreed to that before I had met her—and before I had realized my feelings for Julia. Why don't you just wait things out? Rafael does not love her. Leave well enough alone. They will never marry."

Analisa bit her bottom lip against the tears which came to her eyes. And cursed herself for feeling this way about a man to whom she was less than nothing.

"I don't wish to harm her physically," Carmen cajoled. "All I want to do is discredit her in the eyes of Rafael and Don José. If I could just get her into a compromising situation with Manuel . . ."

"Manuel would never agree. He likes her."

"Manuel would not know," Carmen said triumphantly. "We will just throw them together and let nature take its course."

"Rafael would kill them both. Please, I have no wish to hear this."

"Jaime, darling, you loved me once."

"A lifetime ago. Don't remind me of my folly."

There was a long silence. Then, "If you don't help me, I will tell Julia without batting an eyelash that we were lovers. What do you have to say to that?"

"I was stupid not to tell her in the first place and I intend to do so myself at the first opportunity. She will forgive me, I hope."

"My, my, you really do have it badly, do you not? But before you go, Jaime, I would like you to satisfy my curiosity on one point. You showed no friendliness to Analisa Durant when she arrived, and have not had much to do with her since. Why are you suddenly so protective?"

"I was wary of her, not unfriendly," he corrected, "because of her threat to the security of Julia's future. But Julia already loves her as a sister, and if she feels this way, then I am inclined to believe her. Julia is good at reading people."

"She didn't do so well with you, did she?" asked Carmen.

Analisa heard Jaime sigh. "If you want my opinion, I think she knew what was going on all along, but she loved me and decided to ignore it." She heard him rise to his feet. "And now I am going to return to the veranda, with or without you."

Carmen rose also and she heard their voices fading as they moved toward the house. Analisa sat there a bit longer, mulling over what she had heard. If she hadn't much cared for Jaime before, she thought he was a fantastic person now, and knew in her heart that he and Julia would be happy together. But Carmen—she was something else again. She had almost felt the woman's hatred singeing her through the bushes. A part of her sympathized. What must it be like to have loved a man like Rafael, in every sense of the word apparently, and believe him lost to another woman? Agony.

She rose and resumed her walk. She couldn't do any more thinking tonight. She was afraid of what she might discover.

She wended her way along the path, arriving at the veranda to the chorused "hellos" of those already there. Rafael moved down the three steps toward her and gave her a light kiss on the forehead in greeting. For show, of course, she thought.

His eyes narrowed at the sight of her pale face. "We were getting worried about you," he said, leading her up the steps and seating her in a large comfortable chair. He sat on the stone wall that surrounded the entire veranda and looked down at her. "Angela said you left your room some time ago."

Analisa's eyes involuntarily met Carmen's. "I had some thinking to do and sat in one of the alcoves for a time. I'm sorry if I worried you."

He leaned closer to her and spoke in a tone no one else could hear. "Are you all right?"

She cursed her lower lip for trembling, and Rafael for noticing it. "I'm just fine, considering my whole life is a lie at this particular time."

Don José handed her a glass of dry sherry and took a seat next to her. Manuel joined his brother on the wall, and Jaime and Julia pulled up chairs next to Analisa also so that they were all sitting in something of a circle.

Don José patted her knee. "My daughter tells me the two of you began work on the schoolhouse today. What do you think of the idea?"

"I think it's going to work—and I'm flattered that she wants me in on the ground floor. I just hope I can be some help."

Julia pooh-poohed her. "All the boys will fall in love with your golden hair. You can be sure they will show up regularly."

Carmen sat on the wall next to Rafael and appeared interested in the conversation. "How do you plan on capturing their attention enough to get them to come even on the first day?"

Julia gave Rafael a wicked look. "I thought perhaps if we could get a certain matador who is famous throughout Spain to give a talk the first day on the value of a good education sprinkled with some *corrida de toros* stories, their young imaginations and minds would be truly captured. Every child on this ranch of the male persuasion wishes to be like Don Rafael."

Rafael held up his hand in surrender. "No more flattery, please. I will do as you wish."

Analisa looked over at Jaime and smiled to herself when she saw him gazing at Julia with unconcealed love and pride.

Tía Maria came onto the veranda and smiled quietly as she watched everyone laughing and talking. "Dinner, my loved ones, is served." The table which had been used for breakfast that morning was now covered with a lace tablecloth and set with fine china, silver and crystal. Analisa was again seated next to Don José, but Rafael took the seat on her other side this time. Since the table was circular and smaller, conversation was made easier.

Carmen was between Manuel and Jaime and seemed bent on making Rafael jealous by chattering madly to them. If Rafael noticed, he gave no sign. Between Rafael and his father, Analisa was coaxed into completely cleaning her plate—even though she really didn't require much arm-twisting. She had worked up quite an appetite, and the food was delicious. Tonight, however, she avoided the wine.

The more she was around Don José, the more she loved him. This evening he wanted to tell her stories about old times with her father, and she wanted to hear them. She had heard them all before, of course, from her own father, but Don José had a subtle wit which caused her to laugh all over again at some of the scrapes the two when young had gotten themselves into. She was so absorbed in his storytelling that she didn't see the way Rafael's blue eyes quietly rested on her.

After dinner, Tía Maria and Don José went back into the house, leaving the young people on their own. Jaime and Julia wasted no time losing themselves in the garden. Carmen tried unsuccessfully to get Rafael to walk with her before Manuel dragged her into the house to play a game of pool.

Rafael looked over at her when the others had gone. "Alone at last. I thought they'd never leave."

She looked at him expressionlessly. "And I never thought I'd hear that from you."

"Time changes all things." He sat on the stone wall again and pulled Analisa by the hand until she stood directly in front of him. "Would you like to talk about it?"

Her lip began trembling again. "About what?"

"About whatever is bothering you," he said patiently.

What could she say to him? That she was afraid she was falling in love with him? That should provide his life with some amusement.

"I just hate the lying, the pretending." That was true. But it wasn't all of it. "And I can't help but think about what's waiting for me back in Vermont. Nothing. I have to start all over again, practically. It frightens me."

He looked at her thoughtfully for a moment, then came to a decision. Reaching into his pocket, he pulled out some papers folded lengthwise and handed them to her. "Perhaps this will make things easier for you."

"I don't understand . . ."

"If you read what you're holding," he said wryly, "everything will become clear."

She opened them and gasped. It was the deed to the Vermont estate. She looked up at the Spaniard, speechless, tears coursing down her smooth cheeks.

"Well," he said, amused, "I seem to finally have found something which will silence you."

Slowly, she moved between his legs, put her arms around his neck and lowered her head onto his shoulder. After a slight hesitation, he began smoothing her silken hair with his hand in a comforting motion, holding her close to him with the other. "The gift was supposed to make you happy, Analisa," he said softly.

"It has," she choked. "Oh, it has! But how can I accept it? It cost you a fortune!"

He held her away from him and she suddenly felt bereft. "What is important is not the cost, but the fact that you now have a place to go. You must never feel hemmed in, or obliged in any way. And also, you are doing me a tremendous favor by agreeing to this charade. I know it's difficult for you. When you are back home, and this is all behind you, perhaps you will think of us here once in a while as you wander around your house."

Her eyes searched his carved face, finding a

gentleness there she would never have believed possible. She wanted him to kiss her. More than anything in the world at that moment, she wanted him to kiss her.

There was a question in his eyes as he pulled her slowly toward him, as though he didn't quite understand what was happening either. Their lips met and Analisa closed her eyes against the painful longing which welled up inside her. The kiss deepened. Analisa's fingers tangled in his thick black hair, loving its texture. She pushed thoughts of the charade out of her mind. There was no room for anything but Rafael.

Don José cleared his throat from behind Analisa. She jumped and would have moved away from Rafael if he had let her, but his arms were securely around her waist. "Did you tell her about Pippa yet?" the old man asked.

Rafael looked at his father and shook his dark head. "I'm afraid you just did that."

"Pippa?" Panic replaced passion. "Is she all right? Did the new owner hurt her?"

Rafael smiled at her. "She's here."

"Here? I don't understand. . . ."

"She's in the stables, waiting for you to ride her—tomorrow, not tonight," he added at the look in her eyes.

"But how? Aren't there regulations and things?"

"Why don't you let me worry about that?" he asked her.

She shook her head in wonder. "There just aren't words . . ."

Don José spoke up. "That light in your eyes is

enough." He patted her head and walked back into the house.

Rafael rose and moved away from Analisa to the other end of the veranda, looking up at the sky. "I have a feeling we are going to be in for quite a storm sometime soon."

She looked up at the cloudless sky. "How can you tell?"

"It's just a feeling in the air," he explained. "A quiet." His aloof mask was back in place.

Carmen came back onto the veranda, with Manuel following closely. Carmen looped her arm through Rafael's and smiled over at Analisa. "You won't mind if I steal him away from you for a moment, will you? There are some questions I have about my late husband's estate only he can answer."

"Not to worry, brother," Manuel called cheerfully as he moved to a swinging loveseat. "I will take excellent care of your betrothed in your absence." He patted the empty space beside him. Rafael glared at him but walked off into the gardens with Carmen.

Analisa sat next to Manuel, but her thoughts were following the couple who had just left. Don José stepped out of the house and smiled at the two of them as he crossed to a lounge chair. "Just ignore me, you two. I only wish to stargaze, not to intrude into young lives."

Manuel began to move the swing in a gentle rhythm back and forth. Somewhere in the back of her mind, she realized that the swing didn't squeak like most of them did. She watched Don José who was absorbed by the stars. She couldn't help but wonder how he was going to take the news of the false engagement. She had grown to love him in such a short time. He seemed, at first glance, to be quite strong and healthy, but when one watched him a bit, his frailty made itself known, and it saddened her.

"I must say, it's rather insulting when the girl next to one has eyes only for one's father. I could get some kind of complex!"

She smiled at him. "I have a feeling you've never had that problem before, Manuel."

He grinned broadly. "Now that you mention it, I must admit that most of the women who are lucky enough to sit next to me are aware of me. Why is it that you are so different, I wonder?"

Perhaps it's because I'm in love with your brother, she thought, but pushed it immediately from her mind. Thinking like that, feeling like that, would only bring her grief.

Suddenly something occurred to her. Earlier, when Rafael had kissed her . . . she had thought it was because he had wanted to, but perhaps he had seen Don José walk onto the veranda and kissed her for show. Of course that had been it! The whole thing had been planned! She felt like a fool.

"Manuel," she said suddenly, "would you mind terribly if I went to my room now? I'm very tired."

He looked at her in surprise. "Aren't you going to wait for Rafael?"

"I don't think so. Will you just tell him good night for me?"

"Of course."

She rose and walked over to Don José. "Good

night," she told him softly, leaning over and kissing his weathered cheek.

He gave her a light kiss in return. "Good night, child. I hope you have sweet dreams."

She didn't. They were jumbled and confused, like her life was at the moment. And they were all of Rafael.

Chapter Eight

The next morning, after an early breakfast, she and Julia rode over to the schoolhouse, determined to get some work done before the proposed picnic. Analisa delighted in riding her beloved Pippa again —and Julia was so happy for her one would have thought the whole thing was her idea.

For hours the two girls scrubbed for all they were worth. Julia was just finishing washing down the walls while Analisa was on all fours scouring the floor. When she was three-quarters of the way through, she sat back on her haunches and rubbed her forehead tiredly with the back of her hand, leaving a black streak in its wake. "Whew! I can't remember the last time I worked this hard—or in this kind of heat!"

Julia collapsed on the floor next to her. "Tell me about it! I wish we could have gotten one of the men to help us out. Manuel, for instance, had absolutely nothing better to do."

Analisa smiled tiredly. "Well, just think. When we get home this afternoon we can walk around feeling terribly superior to all those lazy creatures."

"I would have much preferred sharing the load, I can tell you."

"No, don't," Analisa begged. "I'll probably have all I can handle by forcing myself not to kick them in the shins."

Julia looked around the room, now sparkling clean for the most part, and grinned. "We've really done the job, haven't we? This place should be ready for business in no time at all."

Analisa felt a certain amount of pride in what they had accomplished in such a short amount of time. "If our teaching skills are half as good as our housekeeping ones, we're going to have a whole crowd of little Einsteins and Madame Curies."

"Once we talk them into attending class."

"Don't worry. Once they discover what fun learning can be we'll have to lock the doors on weekends!"

Julia reached out and shook her hand. "I believe the two of us shall make a fine team!"

Analisa smiled. "I'm with you. And now, I have to finish this floor." She started to lean forward but sat back again with a groan, causing Julia to laugh. "I knew I shouldn't have taken a break. My scrubbing rhythm is shot all to pieces . . . and my back is killing me!"

"Perhaps Jaime can finish it up later for us?"

"Oh, no! I was only kidding . . . well, half kidding," she conceded at Julia's look. "And speaking of your betrothed—why haven't the two of you set a date for a wedding yet?"

Julia shrugged. "We will, in time. I am, quite simply, not sure enough of him yet. Something has been on his mind lately and it has changed him."

Analisa went over in her mind the conversation

she had heard between Jaime and Carmen in the garden the night before. "Perhaps whatever was bothering him has been worked out by now."

Julia looked at her with narrowed eyes. "What do you know that I don't?"

Analisa started to answer her honestly, but caught herself up. Jaime would tell the woman he loved everything in good time. It wasn't her place to interfere. "Let's just say that I have it from a reliable source that your Jaime is head over heels in love with you."

"And you believe this reliable source?"

"Absolutely."

"And I suppose that even were I to sit here and badger you for half an hour you would tell me nothing else?"

"Right again."

"Then I won't." She rose wearily to her feet. "But don't you think for a moment the subject is closed!"

After another hour of strenuous effort, the place was sparkling. All they needed now were the promised windows and furniture.

They rode home in the incredible heat of an early Spanish summer afternoon, and gratefully turned their mounts over to a man in the stables after nearly falling off them in exhaustion. They were both so tired that conversation was too much effort as they dragged themselves across the lawn and through the back gardens to the shady and cool veranda. Everyone was already congregated on it, apparently waiting for them.

Manuel spotted the stragglers. *"Hola!* There you two are at last. We were beginning to get worried!"

111

The girls stopped at the foot of the veranda, looked at each other then back at Manuel. His eyes widened and he gave a sideways glance at Rafael. "Was it something I said?"

Rafael threw back his head and laughed as he moved down the steps to the girls. "I suspect you are not the only one in hot water." He looked down at Analisa. "And you even have your warpaint on," he told her, taking out a handkerchief and wiping the black smudge from her forehead.

She looked over at Julia with raised brow. "Which shin first?"

"You get the left, I will get the right," she suggested.

"Now, now ladies," he grinned. "Of what use would I be to you maimed?"

Analisa thought it over for a moment. "About the same, wouldn't you say, Julia?"

"No more, nor less," she agreed.

Rafael turned them both toward the steps and helped them up. "I think I'll be safer up here where there are more targets to choose from."

To the chuckles of the others, the girls fell into chairs and closed their eyes. Jaime sat on the arm of Julia's and lightly touched her dark hair. "You had a hard day of it?"

"Don't ask," she groaned.

"But knowing you, it is all finished," he offered, sounding proud of her. He smiled at Analisa. "When my betrothed puts her mind to something, nothing can stand in her way."

"I'm learning that myself from firsthand experience," she told him wryly.

Rafael returned from a corner of the veranda and

handed each of the girls tall, icy glasses of lemonade. "Drink up, ladies. This will revive you."

Analisa let some of the cold liquid trickle down her throat then held the perspiring glass against her hot face. "Oh, that's fabulous! Thank you."

Don José laid aside the book he was reading on the lounge chair. "So, I take it the new schoolhouse is ready to be opened for business?"

"Not quite," his daughter told him. "Rafael is in charge of windows and furniture. Then we will be ready."

"The windows will be in by tomorrow evening and the furniture here within the week. Still wish to kick me in the shins?" he asked his sister.

"Perhaps not quite as much," Julia smiled.

"And you?" He turned to Analisa with just a hint of a smile in his incredible blue eyes.

"I haven't decided yet," she smiled tiredly. She knew he was like this to her simply because there were others around, but nonetheless, she felt closer to him than ever before. She even imagined she saw some warmth in his expression when he looked at her. As a matter of fact, the way he looked at her turned her legs to jelly at times. But eventually the audience always left, and the mask was always put back in place.

She watched him now as he took the chair next to hers, talking to his father about the ranch. He felt her gaze and looked over at her with a lazy smile which did all sorts of strange things to her stomach. Then he reached over and took her free hand in his while he continued his conversation. She closed her eyes and sighed peacefully. If only it could always be like this.

An unnoticed Carmen tearfully headed into the house without a word.

Rafael gave a tired sigh and put Analisa's hand back in her lap. "If you will excuse me," he asked, rising, "I think I should speak with her."

Don José leaned forward and patted her hand as she watched his tall figure disappear from her sight, her peace shattered. "Don't worry your pretty head about it."

She gave him a gentle smile. "You're a very kind man, Don José." She put her own glass down. "If everyone will excuse me I think I'm going to soak in a nice tub of warm water before the aching starts. What time do we leave on our picnic?"

"In exactly one hour," Jaime said looking at his watch.

"Then I'll see you all then. How about you, Julia?"

"A bath sounds heavenly, but I think I'm going to sit out here a bit longer."

"If you need someone to scrub your back—" Manuel offered Analisa.

"Manuel!" his father very nearly shouted at him. "That I should live to hear my son speak in that fashion to his brother's betrothed!"

"I was only joking, father. Well, half joking," he corrected in an undertone.

Analisa just shook her head and went to her room.

Angela smiled at her. "I heard you say you wanted a bath so I have it running for you."

Analisa gave the woman an affectionate hug. "Thank you. You're always so busy taking care of me, I wonder how you find the time to care for your own family."

"I have none," she said simply, not asking for sympathy. "My husband died more than ten years ago. We were never blessed with children."

Analisa began undressing. "Do you live on the estate, then?"

"Only when Don José needs extra help, such as now. Then I stay in the servants' quarters right here in the villa. Otherwise I have my own home in Cordoba."

Analisa stopped what she was doing and looked at the woman thoughtfully. "You sound as though you prefer living here?"

"Oh, I do. I love people. I love working here. In Cordoba it is very lonely for me."

Analisa nodded sympathetically. "I felt that way after my father died. The only time I forgot about being lonely was when I was reading a good book."

"Ah, but not everyone can read." She began picking up Analisa's dusty clothing.

Analisa's smooth brow furrowed. "Are you saying that you aren't able to read, Angela?"

The tiny woman shrugged. "Schooling was considered even less important in my day than it is today. There are many of us, in middle age, who are unable to read or write."

"But that's disgraceful! Something should be done about it!"

"By whom? The government? They are having trouble providing facilities for the young ones, much less we older illiterates."

An idea struck her suddenly. She was definitely

115

going to have to remember to speak with Julia about this problem. There was no reason why they couldn't hold some adult classes in the evenings.

The bath was gloriously refreshing. Her silky blonde hair dried in no time while Angela brushed it in long, gentle strokes. When it came to what to wear, however, she was stymied. She wanted to look nice on the picnic, but Julia had told her that they would be riding their horses. A sundress was definitely out.

Angela walked over to her closet and pulled out a sea-green culotte skirt with a narrow white belt and a matching checked cotton blouse. "What about this?"

"Perfect. Thank you," she said gratefully. "I don't know where my mind is. I forgot I'd even packed that outfit."

"You're just tired from all the scrubbing in this terrible heat."

Analisa slipped into the skirt and blouse. "Speaking of the terrible heat, is it like this all summer?"

"Mostly, unless we have a cooling rainstorm—which is not often, I can tell you."

"Rafael seems to think one is coming soon. He said something about the quiet."

"I agree." She pulled the brush through her charge's hair one more time. "It will probably be here by tomorrow night. There." She stood back and admired her handiwork. "You look beautiful, if I do say so myself."

Analisa's cheeks turned pink. "Watch out or you'll have me thinking you're Irish instead of Spanish."

"You mean blarney?"

"Precisely. Listen, Angela, I don't know what time we'll be back or anything else, so there's really no need for you to sit around here—especially if something more interesting comes up."

"Would you mind very much if I tell you that it gives me pleasure?" she asked quietly.

Analisa sighed. "Well, just a little." She started from the room, then turned back with a crooked smile. "Actually, it gives me pleasure, too. It's almost like having my very own mother after all these years."

She arrived back on the veranda to find that everyone had left but Don José. He rose when he saw her and waved her into the chair across from him. He smiled appreciatively at her fresh appearance. "Ah, to be young, and healthy and in love! There's nothing quite like it so enjoy it while you may!"

"I shall," she assured him. "And how are you feeling today?"

"Better for having you here, child. You bring with you fond memories of days past. But I am a very boring topic. I have been wanting to ask you what you thought of the testing yesterday."

Analisa hedged. "It was certainly different from anything I've ever seen before . . ."

"Which is no answer," the old man teased. "Were you in time to see Rafael?"

"Oh, yes, indeed. He works very . . . close to the horns, doesn't he? Has he had many accidents?"

"Not as many as most matadors, because he is one of the best!"

"Spoken like a truly proud father."

Don José shook his white head. "Being his father

has nothing to do with it. Anything you read about him, written by some of the most noted afficionados in the world, will tell you the same thing."

"I didn't realize. . . ." There was a touch of wonder in her voice. "You see, he never really spoke to me about it."

"Of course not! What could he have said? I am a great matador? It would have meant less than nothing to you. But now that you are here you can begin to learn about the art, for it is that, no matter what some say, and develop an appreciation for the skill and courage required."

A frown creased her forehead. "I understood that he retired from the ring—except for charity fights."

"That is still one fight per month."

Her emerald eyes widened. "Twelve a year! So many?"

Don José laughed. "So many?" he mimicked kindly. "My dear, he used to fight as many as ninety times in a given year!" He studied her face thoughtfully. "That bothers you?"

"Yes," she answered softly. "That's twelve times every year he faces possible death at the horns of a bull. One time is too many."

He patted her hand. "I understand what you are saying, but I hope you will not let Rafael know of this. It is something in the blood, and to ask him to give it up entirely . . . it wouldn't be fair to either of you."

"But . . ." Analisa began when Rafael walked onto the veranda, freshly showered and dressed in thigh-hugging jeans and a blue striped shirt.

He had a picnic basket on either arm which he

placed on the floor before taking the seat next to her. "So, what are you two in such earnest discussion about?"

His father smiled. "I am merely getting to know my future daughter better. Now, tell me. Have the two of you set a date?"

Rafael flicked an imaginary speck of lint off the knee of his jeans. "Not yet."

The old man clicked his tongue. "I don't know, son. If Analisa were my betrothed I would want to secure her as soon as possible."

Rafael looked across at his father and smiled. "Message received." He looked around the veranda. "Where's everyone else?"

"You're the only one I've seen so far." Analisa was looking at Rafael in profile and her heart began the rapid pounding that was becoming so familiar to her. His black hair was still damp, with a tendency to curl slightly. She wanted so badly to touch it that it was an actual physical effort to hold her hand still.

"Here we are!" Julia laughed happily with Jaime and Manuel in tow. "Tía Maria said you already had the picnic baskets—ah, there they are." She leaned over and gave her father a kiss. "*Buenas tardes, papá.*"

"Still happy about the progress of your school, eh daughter?"

"Oh," Analisa exclaimed, "I'm glad you brought that up." She turned to Julia with bright green eyes. "I was talking to Angela earlier and she tells me that there are many adults on the ranch who can't read or write, and I was wondering what you'd think about holding night classes for those who wish to learn."

Julia gave a quick nod of her dark head. "I think that's a wonderful idea. Lots of extra work, but well worth it."

Rafael looked over at Analisa with raised brow. "It sounds as though you plan on staying around for a while," he said in an undertone. "Have you made some decisions you haven't told me about yet?"

"What was I supposed to do?" she hissed back. "You told her I'd be happy to help out—and then didn't bother to mention that fact to me!"

Carmen walked onto the veranda looking stunning, as usual, in formfitting slacks with a matching pink top, and took up a position near Rafael. "Well, are we picnicking or not?"

Analisa's heart plummeted. The last thing she wanted to do was sit through an entire picnic with Carmen glaring at her.

"We are." Rafael rose and pulled Analisa to her feet.

"You children have a wonderful time!" Don José called after them as they all trekked down the steps and through the garden. They split into groups of two with Rafael and Jaime talking intently in the lead, Manuel and Carmen behind them and Analisa and Julia bringing up the rear.

"I hope you realize," Julia told her in no uncertain terms, "that I am going to keep pestering you until I discover what you know that you aren't talking about with regard to Jaime."

"Why, Julia," Analisa drawled in her best southern accent, "whatever are you talking about?"

"Such innocence!"

"What are you two talking about back here?" Manuel asked, slowing his pace. "How wonderfully attractive I am and what a much better husband I would make than Rafael?"

"Dream on, little brother," Julia scoffed good-naturedly.

"Ah, well," he sighed dejectedly. "What is to become of me, in love as I am with my brother's betrothed? What hope of happiness have I?"

Both girls raised their eyes heavenward and groaned loudly.

"All right, all right, I admit to some slight exaggeration—but only slight."

Carmen, who had remained silent up to this point, now added her two cents worth. "You know, golden girl, if I were in your shoes, I would grab Manuel and run."

Manuel decided to turn it into a joke. "For once I must agree with you. What do you say, little sister-to-be? Shall I show up on your threshold in the early hours of the morning and whisk you to a church?"

Analisa was saved from answering by their timely arrival at the stables. Their horses were all ready and waiting. Analisa smiled when she saw Pippa and walked over to Rafael as he secured the picnic baskets on his own huge stallion, Diablo. She lightly touched his arm. "I want to thank you again for bringing Pippa here. I think that's one of the nicest things anyone has ever done for me."

Rafael finished tying the leather strap and looked down at her with a crooked smile on his handsome mouth. "You are a very easy woman to be nice to."

"All right, lovebirds," Manuel called out loudly, causing Carmen's eyes to narrow. "Let's get moving here."

Everyone else was already mounted. Rafael

helped her into the saddle then climbed onto Diablo's back.

They kept a modest pace for the most part. Analisa somehow found herself next to Julia again. "Do you know where we're going?"

"He has been quite mysterious about the whole thing, and frankly, the only thing I know of that's out this way is the old Francisco place."

"What's that?"

"A villa that was once quite lovely, I understand, but is now old and run down."

"Is it on your property?"

"Not at all. There is quite a large portion of land that goes with the villa. As a matter of fact the Francisco's used to be one of the top olive growers in Spain."

Rafael slowed his big black stallion until the girls caught up with him. "What do you two have your heads together about?"

Analisa shook her golden head and looked over at Julia curiously. "Do you somehow get the impression that the Santiago men don't like to see us chatting alone?"

"I do indeed. I wonder why that is?"

Rafael raised a dark brow. "Perhaps it has something to do with the conspiratorial way you look at one another."

The girls looked at one another again and raised their shoulders simultaneously then burst into laughter. Rafael looked at his sister affectionately. "It is good to see you laughing again."

The others joined them. Manuel maneuvered himself to Analisa's side so that she was flanked by

Rafael on one side and him on the other. She knew he was trying to keep Carmen away from her and smiled her appreciation. Manuel smiled back at her, but as he looked at her his brown eyes grew more serious and thoughtful until she had to look away, remembering what Rafael had told her about Spanish men and the thrill of the chase.

Carmen pulled her horse next to Rafael's. "So, where you taking us?"

Analisa's heart contracted when she saw him smile down at the other girl. "You mean you haven't figured it out yet? Unless I miss my guess, Julia is miles ahead of you." He looked across at his sister. "Am I right?"

"The old Francisco place?" she hazarded.

He inclined his dark head. "Point to you."

Carmen wrinkled her dainty nose. "But why?"

"Because you are looking at the new owner. I've had the whole thing repaired, the gardens replaced, the lawns worked on and furniture moved in."

"But why?" Carmen asked astonished.

He looked at Analisa for a long moment then turned his attention back to his questioner. "Because all I really have to call home is my apartment in Madrid. I wanted something here I could call home as well. A place to raise children in. A place to bring a wife."

Carmen's jaw clenched. "But what about your father's home?"

"When Jaime and Julia are married things are going to be crowded enough there."

It took Jaime a moment to realize the full implication of what had just been said. Rafael was seeing to it that his father's property would one way or another revert to his sister . . . and to Manuel, of course.

Before anyone could say anything else, they rode to the top of a small hill which overlooked a wide expanse of lush lawn, groves of olive trees as far as the eye could see, and set right in the middle, a beautiful, white moorish home in all its breathtaking beauty. Rafael watched Analisa's astonished reaction. Words failed her.

"I see I've done the impossible. Silenced you twice within twenty-four hours."

Julia shook her head. "It's splendid. Who would have thought those old ruins could ever look like this?"

"Well let's look at it close up," Manuel said, spurring his horse to a gallop. There was a lovely, tree-lined brick drive which wound its way to the house, and they followed it, almost to the front door. A man appeared from nowhere and took their horses. Two beautifully carved mahogany doors set in an arch swung open and Rafael led them into his new home. Sunlight was everywhere. They went from a wide foyer with a mosaic floor into an enormous living room with white carpeting. Two, not one mind you, but two, grand pianos were set at one end of the room, arranged suitably for the playing of duets.

One wall was made entirely of glass and looked out into a courtyard filled with brightly colored flowers. The couch was circular and sectional, upholstered in a gray-blue and white almost burlap material. An enormous, round, marble-topped coffee table sat in the middle and held an oriental vase of delicate porcelain. The influence of the Orient and even of Africa was very obvious, and somehow managed to create an atmosphere of great elegance —and oddly enough, comfort and relaxation at the same time. The dining room was long and narrow. The center attraction was an ebony oriental dining table which ran the length of the room. Six crystal chandeliers hung from the ceiling. One wall was lined by a giant mirror, which gave the room the appearance of width, much the same as in Don José's home.

The kitchen was large and modernly equipped. The bedrooms were furnished charmingly and comfortably and each had its own bath. The master bedroom was particularly appealing to Analisa. She didn't know whether it was because of the way it had been decorated, or because she could picture Rafael in it. Here, as in many of the other rooms, the carpeting was a thick, lush white, the furniture oriental and ebony. But the other furniture in the room, such as the couch and overstuffed chairs set comfortably at one end, and the bedspread, were gray suede! The whole thing was masculine in flavor without being overpowering. It was a room a woman could be comfortable in as well. But Analisa pushed that thought out of her mind almost as soon as it entered. This room as well looked out into the courtyard.

Rafael came up behind her. "Can you speak yet?"

"Oh yes. It's the loveliest home I've ever had the pleasure to look at. Whoever you marry will be thrilled with it."

"That's very encouraging," he said dryly. "We will have to discuss it later, you and I."

She looked up at him with a question in her emerald eyes and she was sure he would have answered if Carmen hadn't come up to them at that very moment. "I wish you had consulted with me on this, darling. I feel sure I could have been some help."

"I had lots of help, Carmen, but thank you anyway." He turned to the rest of them. "All right, everybody. How about a picnic in the courtyard?"

Analisa had to smile as the girls spread out the checkered tablecloth on the ground and set things up. When the Santiagos had a picnic, they did it right, right down to crystal wineglasses. She was used to paper cups and iced tea or lemonade, with fried chicken and potato salad.

For this picnic, there was wine, bread, sausage and various kinds of cheese. They all sat in the shade of an enormous tree located in the middle of the courtyard and talked about Rafael's latest purchase. Rafael remained silent for the most part, his thoughts elsewhere.

As Analisa watched him, she realized how tired she was of fighting her feelings for him. Rather than admit defeat, she rose abruptly and excused herself on the grounds that she wished to look about some more.

Her feet automatically carried her into the master bedroom. She stood there, in the middle, and looked around. She wondered who would be sharing it with him as the years went by.

"Penny for your thoughts," his deep voice came from behind her, startling her into a gasp.

"You'd be disappointed, I'm sure."

"Let me be the judge of that." He stood before

her and tilted her face up with a finger under her chin. "You have been in a thoughtful mood for most of the afternoon. Is there something on your mind?"

She gave a short, unamused laugh and moved away from him to the window which looked out onto the courtyard. "You might say that. I don't know what's happening to me. I keep getting pretense confused with reality. I don't know if I'll ever get my head on straight again."

He turned her around to face him. "As soon as you get away from Spain your life will get back to normal."

She looked up at him, mesmerized. She couldn't help herself as her hand reached out to trace his mouth, knowing her life would never again be normal. Lonely, yes. Empty. Painful.

He captured her hand in his and kissed her palm. "When this craziness is over, we must have a talk. A long talk."

"About what?"

He smiled down at her. "Things."

"What are you going to do if your father asks you about setting a date for our wedding again? Eventually he's going to get suspicious, you know."

"I'll worry about that when the time comes."

She had so much on her mind and so little time alone with Rafael to discuss things that she plunged right in. "What about Carmen? You apparently didn't tell her that this was just a temporary arrangement, and she is heartsick. Can you imagine how she must feel living in the belief that the man she loves is going to marry someone else?"

"So what would you have me do about that?"

"The only thing I can think of is for you to confide

in her. Tell her that you're not really in love with me and that you have no intention of marrying me."

"And what purpose would that serve but to raise false hopes in her? She has always known that I had no intention of marrying her. Why my engagement to you should be so upsetting to her is beyond my understanding. And why she insists on staying in my father's house is also a mystery."

She stamped her foot at him in frustration. "You can be so arrogant sometimes!"

He raised an eyebrow. "And you can act like a child. Carmen isn't your concern."

"Well apparently she isn't yours, either!"

He grabbed her arm and pulled her toward him angrily. "Stay out of things you know nothing about."

She struggled against his grip, but wasn't strong enough to escape. "Let go of me! There's no one here to impress. I don't know why you followed me anyway."

He dropped her arm immediately and looked at her with cold blue eyes. "You think, when I kiss you—when I hold you—its part of the pretense?"

"Well isn't it? Isn't that what it's all about every time you come within two feet of me?" She was close to tears, and rubbing her bruised arm.

He ran a hand through his black hair. For the first time she noticed how tired he seemed, as though he hadn't slept well lately. The arrogance dropped from him. "Analisa, I . . ."

"There you are!" Whatever he had been about to say was lost when Julia walked in. "We're getting ready to leave, you two."

Without another word, Rafael turned and left the

room. Julia looked at Analisa curiously, but was wise enough not to say anything. One more word and she would have been over the edge.

The trip home was a tense one for Analisa. Carmen was pleasant to her—almost too pleasant. And Rafael was broodingly silent.

Between the exhausting hours she had put in at the school that day, and the picnic that afternoon, she was ready for bed at an unusually early hour that night. She tried to hold up—and so did Julia, but they both ended up giving the sandman his due at around nine o'clock and missed dinner altogether.

Chapter Nine

Analisa was left to her own devices the next day. Rafael was back on the range working with the bulls, Julia and Jaime had gone into town to do some shopping, Don José had locked himself in the study to work on the books, Tía Maria, Manuel and Carmen were nowhere to be found.

She spent the morning in the pool, practicing what Rafael had taught her so far. She really wanted to learn to swim.

Back in her room, she pulled out a murder mystery by a famous British author she had started on the flight to Spain and curled up in a rose-colored overstuffed chair next to her bed. She had been reading for about an hour when Angela walked in and smiled at her. "Nothing to do today, señorita?"

She closed the book and laid it on the end table. "Oh, I'm sure I could find something if I tried hard enough, but to tell you the truth, I started that book days ago and have been dying to find out who did it!"

Angela walked across the room and opened the doors to the garden. "It is a beautiful afternoon, although hot. I think it is best that you are indoors anyway. You aren't used to our sun yet."

"Perhaps." Analisa studied the woman's back for a moment. "Angela, is there anyone you date, or see socially?"

Angela turned and raised an eyebrow at her. "Why do you ask?"

"Am I being too personal?" she asked worriedly. "Just say so if I am and I'll mind my own business."

"Not at all. I was just surprised, that's all. As a matter of fact, I have what you might call a date this evening with Pepe, the gardener."

"How lovely! What are you going to wear?"

"Oh, for heaven's sake. I am much too old to worry about things like that."

"Angela, Angela, one is never too old to worry about something like that!" she chastised affectionately. "You want Pepe to think you look nice, don't you?"

"Well, yes. . . ."

"Then let's get to work! Now think about your wardrobe and tell me which dress you want to wear."

Angela moved away from the doors and sat on the edge of the bed, deep in thought. "I have a blue dress which I bought years ago and never had a chance to wear. It is a sort of cornflower-blue chiffon with simple styling. I am afraid it is the nearest thing I have to a dress suitable for a date."

"It sounds perfect. Do you have it here at the house with you or would you have to go to your own home to get it?"

Angela cleared her throat and looked at Analisa with a hint of mischief in her brown eyes. "I brought it with me in the hope that Pepe would ask me out."

Analisa grinned at her. "Good for you. Have you known him long?"

"Almost thirty years. He is a very nice man. His wife died a few years ago, and like my husband and myself, they were childless."

"And you like him a lot?"

"Enough to go out to dinner with him—and you can get that matchmaking look out of your eyes right now, young lady."

Analisa uncurled herself from the chair and kissed Angela on the forehead. "I love it when you go all motherly on me. Now, let's see here." She began examining the woman's hair. It was in a knot on the back of her head and she could hardly tell anything. "May I remove the combs?"

"Must you?"

"Oh, don't fuss at me. You can always put them back in if you want." When the combs were out, a lovely wave of lightly salted black hair tumbled down Angela's back. "Why it's beautiful! You shouldn't hide it in that bun you wear!"

She took a brush from the dresser and began pulling it gently through the long tresses. She worked with it for a good fifteen minutes before she was satisfied and stood back to admire her handiwork. She turned Angela's head toward the mirror. "What do you think?"

Angela looked at herself wide-eyed. "It doesn't look like me at all."

"Of course it does." She indicated a spot over Angela's right ear. "And I think an exotic flower perched right here would be perfect."

The maid's enthusiasm with her new appearance was growing. "I think you are right. I shall pick one right this minute!" She left the room with a light step.

Analisa put the brush and combs on the dresser then started to follow her out when Carmen came tearing into her room without knocking, looking absolutely hysterical. "You have to come with me. Right now. Right this minute!"

"What are you talking about? What's wrong?" She felt a growing sense of panic. The only thing that would make Carmen act like this was if something had happened to Rafael.

"Please. There is no time to talk now. Even as we speak he could be dying! Come." She grabbed Analisa's arm and started dragging her from the room into the garden.

Analisa dug in her heels. "I'm not moving another step until you tell me what's going on. Is it Rafael? Has he been injured?"

Tears trembled on Carmen's lashes. "A bull got him on the range. He is asking for you. We must run!"

Analisa's heart burst in agony, but her head remained clear. "First we must call a doctor and tell Don José and Tía Maria."

"Do you take me for a fool?" Carmen yelled at her. "Naturally that has all been taken care of." She pulled Analisa's arm again. "We must go!"

Analisa looked frantically around for Angela to tell her but she was nowhere to be seen. She couldn't wait. She had to get to Rafael. Together the girls raced through the gardens and toward the stables. "Wouldn't it be quicker to take a car?" she asked breathlessly as they ran.

"A car would never make it. We must take the horses."

They saddled their own and galloped off across the range, Carmen in the lead. The horses couldn't keep up the pace and soon they slowed to a fast trot. Carmen kept changing direction, but Analisa didn't question her. Her thoughts were all centered on Rafael. He just had to be all right!

After more then an hour of riding, she was thoroughly lost—and so, apparently, was Carmen. They stopped the horses while the other girl looked around bewildered. "You stay here, *yanqui*," she said. "I know he's around here somewhere. I will take a look around and then return for you."

"But can't I go with you?" Analisa asked, feeling completely helpless. "My sitting here isn't going to accomplish anything. If you do find him, you'll only have to come back for me. It doesn't make sense."

Carmen wheeled her horse and glared at her. "Will you kindly just do as I ask? It is bad enough that I must be the one to bring you to him. What else must I suffer?"

Analisa bit back the retort her lips wanted to utter. Carmen was right. It wasn't fair.

She watched as the Spanish girl rode off, disappearing from sight in minutes. There were no trees near, so she sat there in the burning sun, her head unprotected, wearing only the sundress and sandals she had put on that afternoon. She worried about Pippa in all the heat and finally dismounted and removed the saddle from her back.

For an hour she stood there while Pippa grazed, waiting. At last she thought she saw Carmen in the distance. Leaving the saddle on the ground she threw herself on Pippa's back and galloped toward where she thought she had seen her. She was almost there when she realized that her eyes must have deceived her. She began to worry about Carmen now. What if something had happened to her also? And Rafael. She had to get to him!

She put her hand up to shade her eyes against the glare of the sun, and as she did, Pippa shied at something and reared straight into the air. Analisa was caught off guard and was thrown from her back. The last thing she remembered was the sound of a crack as her head hit a rock.

Something cold and wet was being dripped on her face. She opened her eyes, slowly. Painfully. It was dark out. Night had already fallen. And it was raining. Thunder and lightning flashed overhead and the strong wind blew the stinging drops into her skin. Her dress was already soaked and plastered against her. It was so cold! She tried to rise but the effort was too much. She fell back to the ground with a groan and lay there a few moments longer.

She struggled to her feet again in the face of the sharp wind. Her eyes searched the gloom for some sign of Pippa, but the mare was nowhere to be seen. The storm had probably panicked her. She cupped her hands around her mouth. "Pippa!" She waited but there was nothing. "Pippa!" She waited again, but still nothing. "Oh, Pippa," she said softly, near tears. "Please come back."

"Well, there's nothing for it," she said to herself, wrapping her arms around her body as much as she could for warmth, "but to walk." Worry over Rafael had returned. Had the doctor been able to help him?

Was he even alive? And Carmen. She was obviously out there somewhere, probably injured or lost. Otherwise she would have come back for her.

The ground here was rough and rocky and the darkness made it difficult to see except for the occasional flashes of lightning. Several times she tripped and crashed to her knees. She was sure they were a bloody mess but that was the least of her worries right now.

Time and again as she walked tears surfaced, but she forced them back. Now was no time to feel sorry for herself. She had to find help.

How long she walked, she had no idea—only that every step jarred her already aching head. She was so cold by this time that her limbs were numb. A finger of lightning clawed its way across the sky, and the range reverberated with the roll of thunder that followed.

Head lowered into the wind and rain, she began ascending a hill, her feet moving almost of their own accord, one step after the other. Her energy was being sapped. All she wanted to do was sleep to get away from the pain of her pounding head, but thoughts of Rafael and Carmen kept her going.

She waited at the top of the hill for another flash of lightning so she could see what lay below. She didn't have to wait long. There was a creek, swollen with rain, rushing madly over rocks and whatever else was in its way. She cautiously began making her way down the hill in the dark. She was halfway down when her foot caught on something and sent her tumbling into the icy waters below.

Her slight form was immediately caught in the current and swept downstream. The foremost thought in her mind was *don't panic*. Rafael had told her that many people drowned simply because they panicked rather than using their heads. She reached out, desperately trying to keep her head above water and more often than not failing and coming up sputtering and choking, and tried to find something to hold on to. A rock. A tree. Anything that would keep her afloat.

But the current was too strong for her. And she was so very, very tired. She took a deep breath and stopped struggling. Just when she had decided it was all over, her body crashed into something solid, knocking what little wind she had left completely out of her—but she was no longer being carried along. It was a downed tree and she held on for dear life, gasping for air.

When she was able, she pulled herself up onto the tree, which she could now see had blown across the creek making sort of a bridge, and lay there, her sundress in tatters, arms, legs and face scratched and bleeding. After a little while she crawled across the tree to the other side and slid off onto the ground below it.

She lay there on her stomach, her forehead pillowed on her arms, and let the rain slash at her as it would. She couldn't go on. Not another step. She closed her eyes and let oblivion take over.

"Over here!" She heard Rafael's voice as though from a distance. "Bring me some blankets!"

"How in the world did she get way out here?" Manuel asked breathlessly as he handed his older brother the blankets.

"That's exactly what I intend to find out." He pulled Analisa against him, pushing the wet hair off

137

her forehead. Her eyes were still closed. She had no intention of waking up in the middle of this dream. She felt so secure. Some kind of light was shining on her. "Oh, my darling," Rafael groaned, holding her body against his and rocking her back and forth. "What could have happened to her?"

Gently, she was wrapped in some lovely, warm blankets. The rain must have stopped, she thought vaguely, as strong arms carried her and lifted her onto a horse. Rafael climbed up behind her and pulled her back against his chest. She sighed contentedly.

The ride was a long one. When they finally got back to the ranch Rafael carried her in his arms once again. She opened her eyes and smiled up at him. He stopped walking and looked down at her, his blue eyes searching her face. "Are you conscious, Analisa? Can you hear me?"

A frown creased her forehead. She reached up with a hand and touched his haggard face. "This isn't a dream, is it? You really are all right?"

"Of course I am. Why wouldn't I be?"

"Because Carmen said . . . *Carmen!* She's still out there somewhere. You have to find her. She could be hurt. . . ."

The sun was beginning to come up and Analisa could see his face so well. His eyes narrowed. "What are you talking about. Carmen is at the house. Why would you think she was on the range . . . unless . . ." Realization dawned on him.

Manuel came up behind him. "The horses are being taken care of. Is she conscious?"

Analisa smiled up at him. "Yes, she is."

Rafael resumed walking, and he was furious.

138

Analisa could feel the tension in him as he held her. Into the house they came, and were immediately surrounded by Don José, Tía Maria, Julia, Jaime and Angela, all talking at once. Rafael walked past them taking her to her room and laying her gently on the bed.

"Is Dr. Garcia here yet?" he asked as he gently unwrapped the blankets.

"We expect him shortly," Tía Maria explained softly as she gazed sympathetically at Analisa. "Where did you find her?"

"By the creek. And I have a pretty good idea of how she got there. Where is Carmen?"

"Asleep," Julia said coldly. "She wasn't unduly upset over Analisa's disappearance."

Analisa tried to struggle into a sitting position but Rafael held her down on the bed. "Why is everyone talking about me as though I weren't here?" she asked.

"Someone run her a warm bath," he ordered without answering. Angela raced into the bathroom and started the water. "She is shivering."

Don José walked over to her and looked down, clicking his tongue when he saw how scratched she was. "What on earth were you doing out there, child? Why didn't you tell anyone where you were going?"

Analisa was beginning to suspect that something wasn't quite right. Rafael was fine, obviously untouched by any bull. Carmen was here and asleep. Had she dreamed riding onto the range in search of Rafael with Carmen? Why would Carmen have lied to her about something like that? Her numbness was fading and her head was aching painfully again. She

139

gave Don José a shadow of her usual smile. "I'm sorry if I worried anyone. I didn't mean to, really."

He touched her face lightly. "We will talk about it later. Right now you just get some rest."

"Her bath is ready," Angela called from the bathroom.

Tía Maria and Julia began shooing everyone from the room so they could strip Analisa of her clothes and get her into the warm water, but Rafael wouldn't budge. "I know none of you are going to like this, but I am going to take care of her until Dr. Garcia arrives. Please, all of you, leave us alone."

Analisa tried to rise again, this time making it to a sitting position. "Oh, for heaven's sake. I'm perfectly capable of taking a bath alone."

"You will be quiet, little witch," Rafael told her. "And the rest of you will leave."

"This is unheard of," Tía Maria protested, but Don José took her arm and shushed her.

"Come, all of you. Leave my son with his betrothed." The heavy carved door closed behind them.

Analisa gave a tired sigh. "Rafael, I have no intention of taking my clothes off while you remain in this room."

"You have no choice."

"I most certainly do. I'm going to walk into the bathroom, undress in there and soak in the tub." She started to her feet and would have fallen in a crumpled heap to the floor if Rafael hadn't caught her.

He held her close to him. "*Querida,* don't fight me. Not now." His voice was deeply soft. "Tonight I

140

thought I had lost you. I have no intention of leaving you yet, so do not ask it."

Analisa moved a little away from him, feeling a bit shaky. Had she heard him right or was that knock on the head causing her to hallucinate? "I don't have the energy to argue with you. Would you at least hold up a towel for me to hide behind?"

He got one out of the bathroom and held it up for her while she undressed. She took it from him and wrapped it around herself. "You may look now."

He turned back to her. She gasped when he lifted her into his arms and carried her into the bathroom and placed her gently in the soapy warm water. The suds covered her quite nicely and she slipped out of the towel and handed it to him, dripping wet. He left while she soaked. What she really wanted was to close her eyes for a year and never have to open them. Perhaps then the aching would stop.

She tried to think about what had happened to her but couldn't concentrate for any length of time and gave it up as a bad job. She had been in the bath about fifteen minutes when Rafael knocked on the door and came in. "Time's up, little witch." He held out a large fluffy towel for her as she stepped from the water. She was too tired even to be embarrassed as he dabbed her skin dry, trying not to aggravate the scratches which covered her. He then handed her a nightgown and left while she put it on, coming back only to carry her to the bed and tuck her in.

Her eyes closed as soon as her head touched the pillow, but she was aware of Rafael sitting in a chair next to the bed, watching her, waiting for the doctor to arrive. A thought struck her and she turned her head so that she could look at him.

"Rafael?"

He leaned forward and lightly touched her hand. "I am here."

"About Carmen. It isn't what you think, you know."

"And what do I think?" His voice was full of tightly controlled anger.

"She didn't really mean any harm. It's just that she loves you so much."

"So much that she would kill you? That's some kind of love you're describing!"

"I think she only meant to scare me, really. She couldn't have known that I would be clumsy enough to fall off Pippa and hit my head, or that a storm would blow up unexpectedly."

He looked at her incredulously. "Are you defending her? After what she did to you?"

"Of course not! I have no more liking for her than she for me—but I understand why she did what she did. She loves you and I'm a threat—or so she believes. Because you didn't tell her the truth."

A pain shot through her head and she gasped as she tightly closed her eyes. Rafael was next to her immediately, pushing the hair off her forehead, gently touching her face. "Stop talking, woman, and rest. I am about to get angry with you."

Analisa's heavy-lidded eyes looked up at him. "Promise me you won't be too hard on her?"

"Analisa, I . . ."

"Please?"

His mouth gently brushed hers. "I promise. Now rest."

She didn't have to be told twice. She was asleep as soon as her eyes closed.

Chapter Ten

A fever developed as a result of her night in the rain. For days she drifted in and out of consciousness, only vaguely aware that every time she opened her eyes Rafael was right there beside her.

When she finally came fully conscious the first thing she saw was Rafael standing with his back to her looking out into the garden. She watched him for a moment, a gentle smile on her face. She loved him so much.

Almost as though he felt her eyes on him, he turned and moved over to the bed. His strong hand touched her cheek. "Analisa, do you know who I am?"

She smiled at the silly question. "Of course, Rafael. Why would you ask me that?"

"And do you know where you are?"

Her brow furrowed. "In Spain. In your father's home."

Only then did he let out a sigh of relief and smile down at her. "So you really are awake this time. You've been in and out of it for about three days now."

"Three days! What happened?"

He pulled a chair near the bed and sat in it as he

143

spoke. "Dr. Garcia said it had to do with the combination of that knock you took on your head and a fever you developed from being out in the cold rain all that time with nothing but a sundress on. How do you feel now?"

"Hungry," she said weakly. "Very, very hungry."

"Excellent! I'll get you something to eat." He started to rise, but Analisa caught his hand and held him still.

"What have you done to yourself, Rafael? You look awful." And he did. He had about three days' worth of dark stubble on his face, his clothes were rumpled and he had dark circles under his eyes.

"Thank you for your lovely words." He gave her a twisted smile and lightly kissed her forehead. "I will send someone in with some food."

She closed her eyes again until Tía Maria came in with a tray for her. "Rafael tells me you have an appetite," she smiled, helping the girl into a sitting position and fluffing the pillows behind her. "I thought perhaps a bit of broth would be nice, with perhaps some crackers. Nice and nutritious but not too filling." She put the tray on Analisa's lap then took the chair so recently vacated by Rafael.

Analisa sniffed the broth and rolled her eyes heavenward appreciatively. "This smells fabulous. Thank you."

"No problem at all, dear. I'm just happy to see you feeling so much better."

"Rafael told me that I've been rather out of it for a few days. I hope I haven't been too much trouble." She took a sip of broth and a bite of cracker.

"As a matter of fact, you have been no trouble at

all. Rafael wouldn't let anyone but himself sit with you."

"You mean to tell me that he's been in here for three days?"

"Almost without a break. He has gone to shower and rest right now, and asked me to tell you that he will be back later in the day."

There was a knock on the door and Julia's cheerful face poked around the corner. "I heard the good news," she grinned, giving Analisa a kiss on the cheek. "And I must say, you are looking disgustingly well for someone who has been so ill."

Tía Maria clicked her tongue at her niece. "Honestly, Julia, the things you say!"

"That's what makes me so lovable," she quipped back, taking a cracker from Analisa's tray and munching happily. "We've all been worried silly about you, you know," she told the other girl more seriously. "Rafael in particular."

Analisa managed a few more sips of soup and could swallow no more. Her stomach must have shrunk. "Is . . . is Carmen still here?" she asked tentatively.

Julia exchanged a look with Tía Maria. "As a matter of fact, she had some business to take care of in Madrid."

Analisa looked from one to the other of them. "Are you keeping something from me?"

Tía Maria rose from the chair and changed the subject abruptly. "Are you sure you wouldn't like a little more broth, dear? It's quite nourishing."

"Perhaps later."

"All right. I'll be in to check on you. Right now I

think Julia and I should leave you to get some much needed rest."

"But . . ." she protested.

"Come along, Julia," Tía Maria ordered affectionately as she took the tray from the bed.

And just like that they were gone. Analisa wondered briefly what they could be keeping from her, but as it turned out, Tía Maria had been right. She was tired. It was dark in the room the next time she awoke. Rafael turned on a dim light in a corner of the room and sat on the bed next to her. "Hello there."

"Hello," she smiled up at him. "You're looking much better than when I last saw you."

"So are you. Feeling better?"

"Much." She struggled into a sitting position with his assistance. "What time is it?"

"Almost midnight. Father came in to see you earlier, as did Jaime and Manuel. They all wished me to say hello if you awoke yet this evening."

"Thank you. Why are you looking at me like that?" she asked.

"Like what?"

"Oh, like you have something important to say, and would rather not have to. Is it about Carmen?"

He ran a hand through his black hair. "Right first time. I am flying to Madrid tomorrow to speak with her. I have some business to take care of while I am there so I'll be gone about a week."

Analisa studied his handsome face for a moment before lowering her eyes. She felt a little sick. "I understand."

Rafael tilted her chin until she had to look at him. "No, you don't." He gave a tired sigh. "Things have become so complicated. My wonderfully thought-out plan was to have you pose here as my fiancée for a couple of months, until my father was better."

"And now?" she asked quietly.

"And now . . . things have happened between us that I didn't expect." With his finger still under her chin he traced her mouth with his thumb. "I no longer want you to leave. I want you here, with me. And I think you wish to stay. Am I right?"

She nodded, not daring to believe what she was hearing.

He looked steadily into her emerald eyes. "Will you marry me, Analisa?"

That, she hadn't expected. "Well, I . . ."

He placed his finger over her mouth, silencing her. "Yes or no."

"Yes." There was no hesitation in her voice.

His mouth covered hers ever so slowly and she responded with a delicious savoring of precious moments. She had always loved him. How could she have doubted it for a second? He pulled away and looked down at her. *"Te quiero,"* he said softly. "I want you, Analisa."

She wanted him, too, and hungered to hear him say that he loved her—but he didn't. He rose from the bed and paced the room, stopping at the doors leading into the garden and looking outside. "How much do you know about Carmen and myself?"

"More than I want to."

"I'm sorry, but I have to explain things to you so you will understand why I must go to her in Madrid."

Analisa straightened her shoulders as though awaiting a blow.

"Carmen and I have been . . . friends . . . for many years. She knew when the relationship began that I had no intention of marrying her, but apparently that didn't stop her from hoping that I would change my mind. When I left you in Vermont to come back here early, it was to talk to her. To try to explain without explaining, if you know what I mean?"

She nodded.

"She flew into a fury, as I had expected, but she also was hurt, and it is her hurt that I am trying to deal with now."

"Honestly, Rafael, there's no need for you to explain. I don't want to hear . . ."

He moved back to the bed and sat beside her. "There is every need. When I realized what she had tried to do to you—and almost succeeded, I could have killed her. But you made me promise not to be too hard on her. The only way I could do that was not to see her at all."

"You mean you didn't see her before she left?"

"I didn't dare."

Analisa plucked at the covers. "Are you absolutely sure you don't love her?"

He kissed the sides of her mouth and looked deeply into her eyes, his own blazing. "I'm sure." His mouth closed over hers again. Analisa's arms went around his neck and her fingers tangled in his thick black hair. When he touched her like this, she could believe he loved her, whether he said so or not.

He lifted his head and looked down at her with a

great sigh. "Let us be married quickly. After all, we have been engaged twenty-three years already. A long enough time, I think."

Analisa ran her finger from his chin down his strong brown throat to the middle of his chest, kissing the spot where her finger stopped. "Couldn't we . . . ?"

He captured her hand in his. "Little did I know I was getting mixed up with a brazen hussy," he smiled. "I can wait another week before making you completely mine—but only because I won't have to see you every day."

Analisa leaned back against her pillows and soaked up the sight of him. "Will we be living at the villa you bought?"

"If you have no objections. It's ready for us anytime."

Analisa bit her lower lip. "Would it be all right if Angela came with us? To live?"

"Of course, if you like." He looked at her curiously. "Why?"

"Oh, I think she's lonely, and living with us would give her a family, more or less. I think it would make her happy."

He smiled gently at the woman he was going to marry. "That's a wonderful reason. And now I must let you get back to sleep. Are you hungry at all?"

"Not really. I'm too tired to eat."

"All right. Snuggle down." He helped her to slide lower into the bed and adjusted her pillows. "I'll be gone in the morning before you wake so I will say good-bye now. And remember. In one week you will be my wife."

He kissed her on the forehead and started from the room.

"Rafael?" He turned to look at her. "I just wanted to tell you"—she started to say I love you, but changed her mind—"that I wish you a safe trip."

He gave her a smile and a wink and was gone.

But he had said nothing about loving her. He had implied it, but he hadn't actually said it.

Perhaps he just felt sorry for her. She closed her eyes tightly. She had never realized that being in love with someone could be so painful. He said he wanted to marry her, but did he? What was she going to do? When he was with her, it was easy to believe that everything would be wonderful. But when he left, uncertainties crept in and would not be ignored. Heaven help her if she made the wrong decision. Heaven help them both.

Chapter Eleven

The next week passed with incredible quickness, for all that she missed Rafael terribly. She was able to get out of bed the day after he left and her improvement was steady and strong after that. She wondered what he had said to Carmen—and she wondered how Carmen had taken it. Much against her will she could understand just how the other woman felt. To have loved and lost Rafael . . . how horrible.

One morning she was reading quietly in her room while Angela puttered about, when Don José entered, a dress of fine Spanish cream lace over his arm. He reverently handed it to Analisa for her approval. "It belonged to my beloved first wife," he explained. "She wore that gown when we married."

Both Analisa and Angela gasped at the beauty of it. Never had she seen anything so delicately made. She turned to Don José with tears in her eyes. "Are you sure you want me to wear it? Won't it cause you pain to see it on someone else?"

He lightly touched the top of her golden head, his brown eyes smiling into hers. "I wouldn't have offered it to you if it caused me pain. You will make my son a beautiful bride, child. I will leave you to try it on now."

Carefully, reverently, Angela helped her into the dress. It was longer in the back than the front. The sleeves were long and tight and came to a point to the middle of the back of her hand. The bodice was tight, from the pearl buttons which reached all the way up to her neck to just past her slender shapely hips. At that point, the lace was gathered in back to form something of a modest bustle which descended into a beautifully proportioned train. A mantilla and comb of incredible beauty, encrusted with pearls, sat on her golden head and flowed down her back. Angela gasped at the finished product. "When your wedding day comes, you must wear orange blossoms in your hair so that they peek through the mantilla. You will be the most beautiful bride ever in the history of Spain," she told her in raptures.

"Just as long as Rafael thinks so, that's all that matters."

"How could he not?" She helped her out of the gown and placed it carefully on a padded hanger. "Have you called your uncle in the United States? Is he able to come?"

"So far he hasn't been in his office. I'll just have to keep trying."

In the rush to get out invitations, prepare menus and all the other things that had to be done to prepare for a wedding, the schoolhouse was virtually forgotten. The furniture arrived and Julia took care of its placement.

Tía Maria was frantically preparing the house for all the guests, and having a wonderful time doing it. Her eyes seemed to have an extra sparkle in them these days. That particularly pleased Analisa, because she realized it meant that she approved of her joining the family. Tía Maria wasn't very forthcoming, and at times it was hard to read her thoughts, but this much at least was obvious. The day before the wedding, Rafael still hadn't come back. Analisa was getting nervous. What if he had changed his mind and didn't want to marry her anymore? What if he had realized that Carmen was really the woman he loved? These thoughts she resolutely pushed from her mind. It would kill her if he changed his mind.

At dinner that night, Manuel, who had been looking positively glum for days, invited her for a walk in the gardens. She looked to Don José for approval. He looked from his younger son to his future daughter-in-law, then nodded his okay. He knew how Manuel felt about the upcoming marriage, and his heart went out to him. Perhaps Analisa could ease the pain for him.

"So, you are really going to do it," Manuel finally said as they reached one of the wrought-iron benches and took a seat.

"Of course I am. You know how I feel about Rafael."

Manuel turned to her earnestly. "It is not too late to change your mind, you know. For Rafael there will always be other women. But for me—I love you, Analisa. It is something I have not asked for, yet it is something I cannot fight any longer, or hide."

"I love you too," she said quietly, "but as a brother. Can you understand that?"

"I can understand it, but I don't like it. I want you to love me as a man. If you say the word I will take you away from here."

She touched his hand and looked up at him, her

eyes sad. "Manuel, please don't do this. You know I love your brother. There could never be anyone else for me. You're a wonderful man. Any woman would be lucky to have you love her, but I'm not the one for you."

He leaned forward, his hands on her shoulders, as though he would kiss her.

"Please, don't do this, Manuel," she asked quietly. "Don't do anything we'll both regret."

He dropped his arms and sat back in the bench, staring out blindly into the garden. "You are so sure of your feelings?"

"More sure than I've ever been of anything in my life."

"I will leave you to it, then. You have my best wishes."

"Thank you." She studied his handsome profile for a moment. "You aren't really in love with me, you know."

Manuel gave an unamused smile. "I will have to take your word for that. Come. I will walk you back to the house."

She didn't sleep well that night. She wished over and over again that she had been able to say something worthwhile to Manuel. She wondered what had happened between Rafael and Carmen. She worried about whether Rafael would actually show up tomorrow. She wondered where her Uncle Em was because she hadn't been able to get in touch with him. Most of all, she wondered if her father somehow knew what was happening.

The morning dawned bright and cheerful. Angela and Tía Maria showed up with her breakfast on a tray and fussed over her. Julia came in to give her moral support and to deliver some good news of her own. She and Jaime had decided to marry in the near future and had already begun work on their wedding.

Toward the middle of the morning, when, at last, she was alone for a few minutes, Don José knocked on her door. "I have a surprise for you. Someone I think you will be particularly happy to see."

She couldn't imagine who, unless it was Rafael—and the others had already told her that she couldn't see him until the wedding.

"Well?" he asked. "Don't just stand there staring at me. May I show him in?"

Her Uncle Em appeared in the doorway. With a scream of joy, she ran into his arms. The Don smiled as he closed the door gently behind them.

Uncle Em held her away from him and looked down at her, studying her feature by feature. "So, you're really going through with it. Do you love him?"

"More than anyone in the world!"

"And it shows. You look more beautiful than I remembered. Spain must agree with you."

"Oh, it does. It does. But enough about me. What are you doing here? I've been trying and trying to call you. Where have you been?"

"Traveling, my dear, traveling." He sat down in a chair and smiled at her as she sat on the edge of the bed. "Going around the world was something I'd always wanted to do and now I'm doing it. Watching your father die reminded me that I myself was mortal, and I realized that I'd better get cracking or I'd never do all the things I wanted to."

"Well, all I can say is that your timing is perfect. Would you be interested in giving the bride away?"

He inclined his white head. "I'd be honored."

"How long are you going to be here?"

"Til tomorrow, my dear, then I'm on my way again, for another six months."

She leaped up from the edge of the bed and threw her arms around him again. "Oh, I'm so glad you're here!"

Tía Maria and Angela walked into her room. "All right, greetings are over. Rafael has arrived, as have some of the guests. It's time to get you dressed, dear."

Uncle Em rose and bowed very gallantly to the ladies in the room. "As you wish." He kissed Analisa on the cheek. "And I shall see you very soon."

Analisa turned to the other women as soon as he had gone. "I need to see Rafael. To talk with him."

Tía Maria shook her head. "That would be bad luck. A bridegroom is never supposed to see the bride on the day of their wedding until the ceremony."

"But . . ."

"No buts."

The women started to dress Analisa. Her heart was fluttering. Rafael had arrived. And he hadn't changed his mind. When she was almost ready, Angela plucked some orange blossoms for her golden hair and placed them carefully before lowering the veil. Both women stood back to admire their handiwork. Tía Maria tearfully kissed her cheek. "You look absolutely beautiful, child. Rafael will be proud."

Angela kissed her also. "Rafael has mentioned to me that you both wish me to come live with you. I would be honored," she said with a hint of tears in her voice. "I love you both."

Then Analisa was alone, waiting. It was the longest ten minutes of her life. She wanted to run away. She wanted to stay. If it turned out that he didn't really love her, what would happen?

The music began. Uncle Em came for her and began walking her down the hall, through the foyer, the living room and the veranda, into the garden, where the guests were seated and where, most importantly of all, Rafael stood waiting for her, his blue eyes following her unwaveringly as he stood there so tall and darkly handsome in his black tuxedo and white ruffled shirt.

Uncle Em delivered her to her husband-to-be with a charming bow and Rafael accepted her hand with a look which told her . . . nothing. Her heart pounded, but she was determined to go through with it. Having him this way was better than not having him at all. But at the back of her mind she couldn't help but wonder what manner of woman she was that she would think that way.

The vows were read. Analisa took each and every one of them to heart. At the end of the ceremony, when Rafael was told to kiss the bride, he lifted her veil slowly and gazed into her emerald eyes. His mouth lowered to hers in a kiss full of promise of what was to come. He might not love her, but he was definitely attracted to her. He placed her hand in the crook of his arm and led her back down the aisle, now his bride.

Analisa was frightened. How was it possible to feel such love for another? How was it possible?

Congratulations were had all around. She met people from the neighboring ranches who had attended the wedding, all very nice people, received the good wishes of the family members, but her attention was wrapped up in Rafael, trying to figure out what he was feeling. It was impossible.

The reception was lavish, beautiful, and best of all, fun. Everyone danced and had a good time, even Manuel, who seemed entranced with a very lovely Spanish maiden who had attended with her parents. Analisa couldn't help but smile at how quickly his attention had been diverted.

Toward evening the guests began leaving. Her Uncle Em was the last to say good-bye, kissing his niece and her new husband emotionally. "You'd better take good care of her Santiago, because if you don't I'll want to know why."

Rafael put his arm around her waist and pulled her closer to him. "There is no need for concern, Mr. Langford."

He looked from one to the other. "I hope not. Drop an old man a line once in a while. I'd love to hear from you."

Finally it was only family left. Rafael and Analisa climbed into his car amid the shouts of the people who were now her family, and headed for the villa Rafael had purchased. When they got there he carried her over the threshold and up the steps to the bedroom. He set her down just inside the door and looked down at her. "Hello, Señora Santiago."

She gave him a tentative smile. "Hello, Señor Santiago."

He took the veil off her head and the combs out of her hair, letting it fall in golden waves around her shoulders. "You are beautiful."

She gulped some air. "I'm frightened."

"Of me?"

"Of myself. Of being here with you like this."

She was still confused. It felt right, being his wife. But it felt wrong, not knowing how Rafael felt, and she couldn't ask him. If it turned out that he didn't love her, what would she do? She'd rather not know than take a chance.

He pulled her into his arms and kissed the worry from her mind. How could anything that felt so right be wrong? She gave herself up to him. His jacket went over the back of a chair. Her beautiful dress slid to the floor.

They were one. Never more so than now.

Chapter Twelve

The happy, warm days passed into weeks. Analisa was sure that nothing could ever disturb the loving peace she had found. Angela moved in with them and kept house while Analisa spent her days cooking for her husband and helping Julia with the school which was now open and packed with chattering children. There were some problems with his father's ranch and Rafael was trying to get them straightened out. He was busy during the days. At night he headed for his study and did architectural drafting. She had almost forgotten about his bull-fighting until he broached the topic himself one night over the dinner table.

He leaned his elbows on the table and looked at Analisa with a twisted smile. "I had no idea American women were such good cooks."

She looked at her husband suspiciously. "With all the nationalities living there we can pretty well adapt our skills to any cuisine. What are you going to tell me that I'm not going to like?"

"Ah," Rafael sighed, "you know me too well, my Analisa. Come here." He patted his knee. She obediently moved to his lap and put her arms around his strong neck. "I am leaving for Madrid in the morning."

She feathered kisses on the corners of his carved mouth. "Now why would you want to do something like that?" she asked softly.

Rafael smiled and kissed her. "I said nothing about wanting to."

"May I come?"

"I am going to be in a charity bullfight. Still want to come?"

Analisa's back stiffened. "Bullfight? But why?"

"Because I choose to, that's why."

"But something might happen to you! I think it's terrible and thoughtless of you to do that now that we're married! You could be killed."

"Nothing is going to happen to me. I have done this countless times in the past and am still here to tell of it." He traced the delicate line of her cheek. "I would like you to come with me."

Analisa was too caught up in her own fears to hear the plea in his voice. She rose from his lap and paced the cozy nook where they were eating. "I'm sorry. I can't." Her emerald eyes begged him to understand. "I just can't watch you do that. I'm sorry."

The mask she hadn't seen in weeks was pulled over his dark features once again, shutting her out. He rose from the table also. "Very well. I don't know exactly when I will be back. Right now I have some work to do in the study."

Analisa touched his arm. "Rafael, please . . ."

He disengaged himself. "If you will excuse me." She watched his back disappear through the doorway and sat down heavily in the chair he had just vacated. Would this always be a point of contention between them? Should she go with him?

Angela came out to clear the dishes and looked sadly at her. "I could not help but overhear. If you don't mind my saying so, señora, I think you are wrong."

Analisa gave her a wry smile. "I'm beginning to think so myself." She helped clear the little table and followed Angela into the kitchen. "But I'm not ready for that yet."

"Perhaps by his next fight you will be."

"When is that?"

"In two weeks at the ring in Sevilla. It's only a forty-five minute drive from here. You might wish to surprise him by showing up."

She rinsed while Angela stacked the dishwasher. "Well, that gives me two weeks to prepare. If you keep giving me verbal encouragement, I just might make it."

"I shall keep up my end." They finished cleaning the kitchen. Angela wiped her hands on the dish towel. "Are you teaching the adult classes this evening?"

"I certainly am. Would my prize pupil like a ride to the schoolhouse?"

Angela blushed delicately. "Thank you. I will be ready in a minute."

This was something Analisa looked forward to. Everyone who attended these night classes really wanted to learn—or else they wouldn't be there. And they learned quickly. Already, in just a few weeks, they had made great strides. Angela in particular.

When they arrived back home around eleven

o'clock, Rafael was still closed in his study. Analisa went to their room and put on a nightgown. She sat up in bed with a book, determined to wait up for him. She didn't want him to go away angry with her.

But all her good intentions were for naught. It was morning when she awoke. The book she had been reading was now on the end table, put there by Rafael probably, and he was nowhere to be seen although his side of the bed had been slept in. She pushed back the covers and padded around barefoot to his closet. Some of his things were gone, as was his suitcase. He had left and they hadn't made up.

The next few days dragged by endlessly. His fight, she knew, was on Sunday. All that day she waited for news of his fate. She spent some time at Don José's, chatting with the family and helping Julia plan her own wedding. It passed the time.

When she got home there was a cryptic, hand-delivered note waiting for her. "As you can see, little witch, I am still in one piece. Rafael." With the note in her hand, she raced through the house looking for Angela. She found her sitting in the courtyard. "Where did this come from?" she asked breathlessly. "Is he back? Is he here?"

Angela smiled. "To take your questions in proper sequence, a messenger delivered it. No. No."

Deflated, she sat down on one of the wicker chairs. "I wonder when he'll be back."

"When his business is concluded and not before, I should imagine."

Analisa took the note and held it against her cheek. "You know, if I didn't love him so much I might be annoyed."

Angela put down her sewing and looked at the

girl. "Have you made a decision about the fight in Sevilla a week from today?"

"Yes. I'm very nearly, almost absolutely sure that I'm going. But don't say anything to Rafael. I want it to be a surprise."

"You still don't sound too definite."

Analisa looked at her in exasperation. "I'm trying, Angela. These things take time, you know."

Analisa didn't see Rafael before his Sevilla fight, but he did call the night before. And he sounded terrible. He had the flu.

She felt her stomach give a leap of fear. "Shouldn't you cancel your fight for tomorrow then? I mean, if you aren't feeling well."

"Analisa, let's not go through this again."

"Rafael, I'm not trying to start an argument. Really. I'm just worried about you."

"Well you can rest easy. I'll be fine. And I'll be home tomorrow evening. We need to talk."

"Yes, I know. I hated your going away without saying good-bye."

She heard him sigh at the other end. "I wasn't too pleased with that myself. Are you all right?"

"I'm fine—except that I miss you terribly."

"And I you. Take care, *querida,* and I will see you tomorrow."

"All right," she said softly, caressing the receiver long after he had hung up. She ached to see him. And see him she would. There was no question in her mind any longer about attending the fight in Sevilla tomorrow. She would be there.

She called Julia to see if she wanted to go. She did. As did Jaime. Manuel had a date with a pretty

Spanish girl he had met at the wedding, so he couldn't make it.

The next morning the three of them set out for Sevilla in Jaime's little car, Analisa taking her cue from the others and joining them in song. They had left early so that they could show Analisa some of the sights of Sevilla which was located about forty-five minutes drive from Cordoba. It was a beautiful little town, very Moorish looking, with narrow streets and white buildings. There were outside cafés with delicious food to tempt the trio.

Bright flowers were everywhere, and smiling people. Analisa wondered what Rafael was doing at that very moment. She had done some reading about how a bullfighter prepares for a fight. It was all very elaborate.

They took her to the most famous landmark of Sevilla, the Giralda Tower. This was a Moorish minaret of the twelfth century which was allowed to remain because the added belltower in the sixteenth century adapted it to the Christian faith. The three of them climbed almost to the top, up an incredibly steep ramp. There was a superb view of the city from up there. From her vantage point Analisa realized what a large city Sevilla really was.

"We started out in the *Barrio de Santa Cruz*," Jaime explained. "That is the old Jewish section of the city and the most beautifully maintained. Now you are seeing how crowded this place really is. It isn't all the charm of the balconies, flowers and half-hidden courtyards, although some feel this charm extends to other parts of the City."

They were still at the top of the belltower. Julia

looked over at her fiancé. "How would you feel about carrying me down?"

"Very unhappy," he grinned. "But look on the bright side. Getting down will be much easier than getting up here was."

"My hero," she said, "well, we might as well start. We still have much to show Analisa before the fight begins."

Jaime was right. The descent was much less strenuous.

Between the two of them, Analisa was sure she had been dragged to every historical building in the city—which was no small feat. At about six o'clock they took her to the bullring. It was attractive, but unspectacular. Analisa could feel herself tense as they joined the throng of people entering and found their way to their seats.

Luckily they were on the shady side, close to the ring itself, and had a very good view. Analisa strained her eyes looking for Rafael but found no sign of him. Julia touched her arm comfortingly. "He's here, and he's fine. Don't worry. Just enjoy yourself."

"I have a feeling the last thing I'm going to do today is enjoy myself."

"Come on," Jaime cajoled. "It is not so bad. And he has done this many times before. Everything will be fine."

She shook her head. "Some women fall in love with attorneys, doctors, musicians. Men with nice safe occupations. But not me. Oh no, not me. I have to fall for someone who fights bulls." She was silent for a moment. "How about if I wait in the car and you tell me how things turn out?" She started to get up but both Jaime and Julia pulled her back down.

"You would disappoint your husband in this way?" Jaime asked.

"But he doesn't even know I'm here, so he won't be hurt that I left. Right?"

"If I have to tie you to the bench to keep you here, I'll do it," Julia told her. "Now relax. The procession is about to begin."

Analisa watched as some men in sixteenth-century costumes entered the arena on horseback called, as Julia informed her, *alguaciles*.

"This is called the procession of the *cuadrillas*," Jaime said. "The matadors are next, then the *banderilleros,* and then on horseback, the *picadors.*"

Analisa's eyes searched the arena for a glimpse of her husband. Suddenly he was there, dressed in what she was told was a "suit of lights." He and the two matadors who walked with him were in short jackets, waistcoats and knee-length, skintight trousers of silk and satin, richly embroidered in gold, silver and silk. They also had on dress capes of satin, heavily embroidered in gold, silver and silk, or combinations of them, which, as Jaime explained, were worn only during the entry procession. A hand-drawn linen lace shirtwaist, coral pink, heavy silk stockings, flat, unheeled black slippers and *monteras,* or hats made of tiny black-silk chenille balls hand sewn in special designs on heavy buckram, finished their outfits.

Rafael looked so handsome! For a moment she forgot why he was there and what might happen to him. She had missed him so much!

The *banderilleros* wore similar garments, lacking

only the gold embroidery which is reserved exclusively for the matadors. The *picadors* wore broad-brimmed, low-crowned, heavy, beige-colored hats called *castorenos,* jackets and waistcoats similar to those of the matadors, but not as ornate, hip-to-ankle armor of steel one-eighth inch thick on the right leg, and knee-length left leg armor covered by tightly fitting trousers of heavy cream-colored chamois and heavily protected chamois ankle boots. This, Julia explained, was to protect him from the horns of the bull. The *picadors'* horses also wore protective armor, much as she had seen at the testing, to avoid any possible harm to the creature.

After the opening procession crossed the arena, the mayor threw down to one of the *alguaciles* the key to the *toriles,* or bull pens. The *cuadrillas* not performing with the first bull left the arena, and the others took their respective positions. Rafael apparently had not drawn the first bull.

As the bull passed through the *toril* door, an attendant perched above attached a silken rosette made of the ranch colors into the shoulder muscles. A *banderillero* caped the bull with one hand only so that the performing matador might judge whether the bull showed marked preference in the use of either horn or attacked equally from both sides.

Analisa watched breathlessly as the matador performed some beautiful passes, or *quites,* with his cape.

"This fellow is good," Julia told her, "but nothing when compared to Rafael."

Analisa, much against her will, found herself fascinated. The bulls were vicious looking, and she couldn't imagine going near one, much less in the same ring with no more protection than a flimsy piece of cloth.

The *picadors* finished their act on the horses and then the *banderilleros* began theirs, on foot. The two men alternated in planting two to four pairs of *banderillas*. These were seventy-two-centimeter staves decorated with colored paper and with a three-centimeter barb at one end which the men placed in the bull's shoulders at the junction with the neck. They did this by attracting the bull's attention with violent gestures and shouts from a distance of twenty yards. When the bull charged the man ran forward and slightly to one side, and as both came together, and when Analisa was sure the bull would crash into him, he deftly planted the staves and spun away to safety. The bull's momentum took it out of goring range.

Analisa's breath came out in a rush. "Why do they do that?" she asked Jaime. "Doesn't it hurt the bull?"

"The purpose behind the *picadors* and *banderilleros* is to weaken the great neck muscle of the bull so that he will lower his head. Believe it or not, that bull's head and neck are so strong that he can easily lift a horse and rider completely off the ground and toss them ten feet."

Analisa put her hand over her pounding heart. "Oh, merciful heaven. And Rafael will be out there with one of them!"

Jaime patted her hand. "Stop worrying."

The entire fight, from start to finish took no more than twenty minutes. The next one began and went much the same as the first. The men were very good with their capes, but the bulls never came within a foot of them.

Rafael entered the arena. It was his turn. Analisa bit her lower lip and determined that under no circumstances would she scream. Little did she know what she was about to see. Somewhere in the back of her mind she remembered that he didn't feel well.

The trumpet blew. The *torilero* jerked the rope that clanged open the heavy gate, and out blasted the bull. It was a monstrous creature. The crowd ooooooooooooh'd.

Analisa grabbed Julia's arm. "Why is this one so much more horrible looking than the other two?"

Julia was tense also. "I guess he lost the draw."

Rafael studied it as it charged viciously against a *burladero* and sent the top slats splintering into the air. One of his *banderilleros* started to go out to give it some testing passes, just as had been done for the other matadors, but Rafael waved him back with a cut of his hand. "Hide yourself!" he ordered.

He stepped out further into the ring and stood there. For the first time, Analisa could see that he really was sick. He looked ready to collapse. She was afraid to look. Afraid not to.

The bull spotted Rafael and lowered his head, starting across the ring toward him. He collected himself, and taking the cape in one hand, dropped to his knees.

"Toro," he called, swirling the cape out flat on the sand in front of him. His voice was mocking. "Hey, little bull, why don't you try charging around this way?"

As the bull thundered down on him, Rafael

watched it come, his face resigned, as though he were simply too tired to get up and jump out of the way. The huge creature looked as though it was going to crash into his chest. Analisa's hands clutched the edge of the bench until her knuckles were white. This couldn't be happening. . . .

When the bull was four feet away, Rafael suddenly swung the cape over his head, flashing it from the left side to the right. The bull veered off its course after the flare of cloth and the animal's right horn grazed by his right eye.

A roar came from the crowd. Analisa's breath escaped in a gasped sob, only to be drawn in sharply again as he stayed there on his knees and did five incredible, liquid passes, so close that each time man, bull and cape made a beautiful blur of gold and black and magenta.

Analisa looked over at Julia and saw that her face was drained of all color. "He's crazy!" she said harshly. "There is no need for this. . . ."

Soon the plaza was a sea of white handkerchiefs and shouts of approval. When the act of the *bande-rilleros* came around, Rafael decided to place the barbed sticks himself. Analisa watched in horror as he ran at the bull as it charged, arms high, his chest only inches from the horns, and finally spinning to one side to let the bull hurtle by.

He picked an impossible way to place the second pair: with his back against the fence. He incited the bull and stood there calmly watching it bear down on him. When the animal was two feet away, Rafael raised his arms, dropped the *banderillas* in place and ducked to the side. The left horn grazed his waist as the bull crashed by.

The trumpet blew for the final phase. Rafael faced the crowd looking utterly exhausted, his small *muleta,* or red cape, and curved sword in his hand. He didn't know that Analisa was there, shaking so hard her teeth were chattering. It was 110 degrees in the stands and she was unbelievably cold.

His first pass was the deadly Pass of Death. Rafael called the bull from twenty feet away, and as it thundered by he remained absolutely motionless and straight, letting the bull choose whether he was going to crash into the cloth or into his legs. Still motionless, and without even looking at the animal, he let the bull wheel and charge again. And again and again, without moving an inch. Time after time he willed that bull into taking the cloth instead of his body, and time after time he should have been killed. The crowd had stopped cheering. They sat in hushed silence, broken only by soft exclamations on drawn breaths.

The next pass he chose to show them was one done by very few matadors because of the danger involved. He flipped the *muleta* around behind his back and offered the bull only a small corner of the cloth that protruded. When the audience realized what he was going to do they began to chant, "No, no, no!" Analisa, Julia and Jaime all joined hands, terrified for him.

The bull charged. Rafael went up on his toes, his stomach sucked in, and as the horn knifed by it caught on the inside of his jacket and ripped it open. But he wasn't hit. He immediately crowded the bull, the *muleta* still behind him, and sighted the animal for yet another pass. This time the bull got only half-way through the charge before lunging to the left.

Analisa and every other man, woman and child in the crowd screamed as Rafael went up into the air, not high but clutching onto the horns of the animal, clinging to its tossing head, and then spinning on the right horn. Somehow when his body slapped the ground, he was stretched out under the bull, the length of his body between the animal's front legs and his head between the lowered horns. People hid their eyes for there was no time for his helpers to get there and lure the bull off him. Analisa leaped to her feet, her fist crammed into her mouth to stop the screams that were tearing her throat.

Before the points could find the inert form, Rafael reached up and locked his arms around the bull's neck in a frantic grip. The bewildered bull spun around and around. Finally it gave its neck a great snap and flung the man from him like a rag doll to the ground ten feet away. But before it could charge, Rafael's men were between them and attracted the bull's attention. Rafael got to his feet and stood there swaying, bruised and dazed, his uniform jacket in ribbons, but miraculously not wounded. He picked up his sword and the *muleta*.

"Get out of the ring!" he yelled at his *banderilleros*.

The men didn't take him seriously and stayed there, ready for any emergency. Rafael repeated the order.

The amazed men retreated several feet behind him.

Rafael whirled on them. "I said leave me alone with him!"

"What is he doing?" Jaime asked incredulously. "He is a madman!"

When they had all left the ring, he turned to the bull who was pawing the ground and studying him ten feet away. Rafael dropped to his knees. He stared into the bull's hot eyes. Then he began to inch forward toward the animal. Closer and closer he came. The bull shifted his feet and the crowd gasped, sure that it would charge. But it didn't; it was as though it were hypnotized and cowed by the enormous brute courage of this man-thing on its knees. Rafael pressed closer, staring fixedly at the bull until he arrived at its very face.

Then, with the muzzle of the bull almost touching him, he leaned forward toward the animal and rested his elbow on the bull's forehead! Then he rested his own forehead on the bull's right horn! Then he took the horn tip in his teeth! A sudden lunge and the horn would have spiked out through the back of the man's head.

He turned around and stared up at the crowd with the bull's nose against his back, a horn jutting out on either side of his head. No one screamed for fear the noise would make the bull charge, but when he faced the bull again, and, still on his knees made it pass by four times, spinning in against the shoulder each time, a great roar burst forth.

Analisa couldn't take any more. She crashed her way across the rows of people and ran as fast as she could out of the arena. She felt sick and frightened and hollow. She had to get away from here! Loving a man the way she loved Rafael and knowing that he could die a horrible death on the horns of a bull at any time . . . she couldn't take it! Her life would be a living hell.

A great roar went up from the arena behind her, signaling the end of the fight and the success of the matador. Analisa dropped to her knees with a sob of thanks.

Rafael was alive.

She felt Julia's arm around her shoulders. "He is all right. There is no need to worry. Come back with us to greet him."

Analisa rose to her feet and wiped away the tears. "I can't, Julia. Please forgive me, but I just can't face him right now." She rubbed her balled fists into her forehead. "He almost died out there!"

"But he didn't!" Julia pointed out. "He fought the fight of a lifetime! You should be proud!"

"Oh, I am! But if I saw him right now I don't know whether I'd throw my arms around him or choke him to death for what he just put me through. I can't let him see me like this."

"He will be hurt, you know." Julia looked at her sadly.

"I know, and I'm sorry, but it can't be helped. When we married I didn't realize what a strain his bullfighting would put on our relationship. I came to him unprepared. I realize now that I'm going to have to readjust my whole way of thinking and learn to accept it or destroy both of us. I have to get away and think things through, and come back to him as the wife he needs."

Julia's brown eyes widened. "Come back to him? Are you going to leave him?"

"Only for a short time. Only because I love him so much," she said softly. "I'd appreciate it if you'd tell him for me. I could never get all of this into a note."

"Then why don't you wait and talk to him yourself?"

"Because one word from him and I'd stay and things would go on the same, with Rafael fighting bulls once or twice a month, and me hating it and taking it out on him."

They could still hear the shouts and applause from the arena. "Very well," Julia finally agreed. "I will tell him what you have told me. However, much against my will. I understand what you are saying, and perhaps your solution is the best one. Where will you go?"

"Rafael bought my old house in Vermont for me so I think I'll go there. It's lovely and peaceful there this time of year."

"May I tell him?"

"Yes, of course. As a matter of fact, I'll leave him a note explaining where I've gone. If he isn't too furious with me perhaps he'll call."

Julia leaned forward and kissed Analisa's cheek. "Don't stay away too long. We will all miss you. Now wait here for a moment while I find Jaime so we can take you home."

Analisa caught her arm as she would have turned away. "No, please, I'd much rather take a taxi. I know it's a long way, but it will make things easier for me. I don't think I could go through this explanation twice, and Jaime will need to know what's going on."

"Yes, of course. You are right. But I hate to think of you taking a taxi alone all that way."

"Don't worry," Analisa smiled thinly at Julia, "here's one now!" She flagged it down, and gave

Julia a hug. "I'll see you in a few weeks. Please don't worry about me. And . . . and tell Rafael that I love him with all my heart and not to be angry."

"Good-bye, little sister. I shall explain everything to him, and Rafael, being the man he is, will understand. Now go before the driver takes off without you!"

The driver's eyes lit up when Analisa told him where she wanted to go. She sat in the back of the rattling taxi and waved at Julia, who stood there waving back until the cab was out of sight.

The bumpy drive lasted almost an hour. The first thing she did on arriving at her own home was call to make arrangements for her trip. She searched all over for Angela, but she was nowhere to be found. Rafael would have to explain things to her.

In the bedroom, she got out a suitcase and overnight bag and randomly picked out some clothing to take with her. She didn't really care what she packed. That done she placed the suitcases next to the bedroom door and sat down at the lovely French writing desk Rafael had bought for her, taking out stationery and pen. She chewed the end of it for a moment before tearfully beginning:

Rafael,

By this time Julia has probably explained things to you. Watching you in Sevilla today I realized something for the first time that your father tried to explain to me. Bullfighting is as much a part of you as breathing. I died inside every time that creature came near you.

I also came to the realization that I can't live

even one day a month wondering if this will be the day that someone comes knocking on the door to tell me you were killed on the horns of a bull. And that brings me to the reason I have to leave for a while. If we are to live and love together I must change that attitude or I will make our lives a living hell. You see, Rafael, you are as much a part of me as breathing.

I have reservations on the 12 o'clock flight out of Madrid and will be in Vermont. Please call me there, and try not to be too angry with me.

Give my love to your father—and to Angela. I couldn't find her.

Take care of yourself.
Analisa

Tears trailed her cheeks as she folded the letter and placed it in an envelope with Rafael's name on it and propped it against his pillow. She looked long and sadly around the room where she had discovered the wonder of loving and being loved, then stiffened her shoulders and picked up her bags.

She drove the little car Rafael had given her to the airport in Cordoba and paid a young man handsomely to drive it back to the villa for her. Then she caught a small commercial flight to Madrid where she was to catch her main flight to the States. Unfortunately, the commercial flight was late and she missed her connection.

The reservations clerk was sympathetic, but there was really nothing she could do but book her on a later flight. The clerk looked down at a boarding list she had in her hand and shook her head. "You know what's strange? We have you down as having boarded that flight, Señora Santiago. I wonder how that happened?"

Analisa shook her golden head. "I'm afraid I don't know. Does it present a problem?"

"Not at all." She set it aside and smiled at her. "We never really use these lists anyway."

Analisa looked around for a place to while away the next three hours, feeling rather lost. "There's a lovely little restaurant down the corridor and to your left, and they don't mind a bit if you sit around while you wait for your flight," the girl suggested.

"But I'm not really hungry. . . ."

"Then just order a salad or something. They don't mind. Really."

Analisa picked up her shoulder bag. "Then I guess that's what I'll do. Thank you for your help." She found the restaurant in question and ordered a small salad.

The small table she chose was toward the back of the dimly lit place. She wasn't really interested in reading anything so she people-watched. What place better than an airport to people-watch?

While waiting for her flight she changed her mind a hundred times. No, she wouldn't leave. Yes, she would. Back and forth. She wanted to feel Rafael's strong arms closing around her again. She wanted to hear him tell her in that deep voice of his that he loved her. But more importantly, she wanted to come to him a woman ready to handle anything, even his bullfighting. A woman he could be proud of. A woman worthy of his love. Why, oh why, did things have to be so complicated?

* * *

Her flight home was uneventful. A cab dropped her off in front of her old home and she stood there for a while, just looking at it. She felt as though she had been away for years rather than months.

Inside things were just the way she had left them, only a bit dustier. She left her luggage in the hall and went directly into the living room to lie down on the couch. She had been feeling rather ill during the trip. "No," she said aloud. But then again . . . it was possible that she was pregnant.

After half an hour's rest she felt much better. She carried her luggage upstairs and unpacked, then slipped into the shower and a nightgown. She didn't even have the energy to eat . . . which was just as well considering there was no food in the house anyway.

Days, and then weeks slipped by, and Rafael never once tried to call her. Could he possibly be so furious with her?

She attempted to contact her Uncle Em, but his secretary told her that he planned to be out of the United States for at least two more months, and there really wasn't any way to get in touch with him.

A hundred times her hand reached for the phone to call Rafael, and each time she pulled back. He knew where she was if he wanted to talk. She ached for the sound of his voice, the touch of his hands, but she was no nearer resolving her own insecurities about his bullfighting than she had been when she arrived.

By the time a month had passed, she developed

morning sickness, and knew, now, that she was going to have Rafael's baby. This was confirmed by the old family doctor. She was filled with joy at the thought.

When she came back from her appointment, she sat in the living room and lightly touched her still flat stomach, amazed that there was actually a little life inside her, created from the love she shared with Rafael. Suddenly all confusion left her. She belonged with the man she loved, no matter what the future held. She wanted to revel in the time they had been given to share. If something happened to him—well, then something happened, but she would have the memories to hold on to. And his child.

This time when her hand reached out for the receiver, there was no hesitation. The operator put through her trans-Atlantic call and in an amazingly short period of time she heard Angela's voice answering the phone.

"Hello, Angela," she said happily. "This is Analisa. Is Rafael at home? May I speak with him?"

There was silence at the other end, then an outraged sob. "How dare you play this cruel trick! Who are you?"

Analisa was shaken at the fury in her friend's voice. "It's me, Analisa. Is something wrong? Can't you hear me?"

The connection was remarkably clear. She heard Angela cover the receiver and speak with someone, then Rafael's angry voice over the line. "What's going on here?"

Her heart gave a leap of joy at the sound of his voice. She had missed him so much. "Rafael, it's

Analisa," she said tentatively. "I . . . I just wanted to tell you that I'm coming home. That is, if you still want me."

There was a sharply indrawn breath at the other end of the line. Then, hoarsely, "Analisa? My God, Analisa! Where are you? Why didn't you call? Your plane—we all thought you were dead!"

"Dead!" she gasped. "Whyever did you think that? Didn't you get my note?"

"Of course I got it. That's one of the reasons . . . the note said you were going to be on the twelve o'clock flight. It crashed with no survivors. You were listed as having been aboard."

"Oh, no! I'm so sorry. . . . I had no idea. . . . I missed that flight and had to take a later one. I haven't read a newspaper or even turned on the radio since I got here."

"Analisa, I want you to listen to me and listen well. I'm catching the next flight out of Madrid. Don't you dare move from the house. Understand me?"

"But that's what I was calling about, darling. I want to come home to you. There's no need for you to . . ."

"So help me, woman, if you dare to argue with me now after what you have put me through I will reach through the telephone line and throttle you!"

"Yes sir," she said meekly. "I'll stay right here."

"I mean it."

"I'm staying here, I told you."

"And Analisa?"

She was near to tears at the way he was snapping at her, and her voice was quiet. "Yes?"

"I love you." Then he hung up.

She held the receiver out from her face and looked at it in astonishment and happiness. "I love you, too," she told the already disconnected line.

That night and the next day passed so very, very slowly she was beginning to think it was a plot. Around ten o'clock she brushed out her long shining hair and put on a cream silk robe. She was afraid to go to bed for fear she wouldn't hear him. She went into the living room and lay down on the couch. She slept so soundly that she didn't hear him walk in and stand there, staring down at her in the dim light. Then he reached out a dark hand and gently touched her smooth cheek.

Analisa stirred at the contact and opened her emerald eyes. She sat up abruptly. When she saw who it was she threw her arms around him. His strong arms closed around her as though he'd never let her go and his deep voice kept repeating her name. He kissed her cheek then pulled back so he could look at her. Analisa stared at him. He had lost a little weight, and now there was white hair mixed in with the black at his temples and sideburns. She reached out and touched it, and started to say something, but he touched his hand to her mouth to silence her, still studying her feature by feature. When his mouth finally closed on hers she melted into his arms, wanting to get closer and closer. She had missed him so. He rested his forehead against hers, his voice affectionately teasing. "First, *querida*, I'm going to make sweet, sweet love to you. Then I'm going to beat you senseless for the unutterable agony you have caused me."

"And all this time I've been sitting here wondering why you didn't at least call me," she said softly. "I can't tell you how sorry I am."

He gave her a twisted smile. "I know you would never have done something like that intentionally. But you will have to forgive me if I never let you out of my sight again. I don't think I could live through it twice."

"Now you know how I feel about your bullfighting," she couldn't resist throwing in. She could have kicked herself when he rose from the couch and walked away from her. He lit a cigarette, his back to her.

"Yes, I do. I have done nothing but think about it since you left, and you will be happy to know that I have decided to give it up, completely, except for occasional gatherings on the ranch."

Analisa moved behind him and place her hand on his broad shoulder. "But you can't! You see," she moved in front of him and made him look at her, "I've done a lot of growing up this past month. I can handle it now, really I can! What's important in our relationship is not that you face death so often, but the love we share. Don't you see? What we have is so very, very precious that to risk it by asking you to forfeit something you grew up with, something that has been so much a part of your life, would be sheer stupidity, and you'd grow to hate me. I couldn't bear that. It would kill me."

He stubbed his cigarette into an ashtray and pulled her into his arms, resting his chin on top of her silky head. "I understand what you are saying, little witch, but you are wrong. When I thought you were dead—and it frightens me to think it took something like that to bring me to my senses—I realized exactly what I had been risking those days in the bullring. Losing you. And I knew that it wasn't worth it." He held her away from him and looked intently into her eyes. "I love you so much. And have for so long."

"For so long? I don't understand."

He smiled at her. "I was twenty-three when I met a ten-year-old girl with a rotten temper who nearly maimed me for life, and I never forgot her. I fell in love with the woman I knew that girl would become."

She looked at him in wonder. "All that time? But why did you try so hard to hate me when we met again?"

"Because of the Spaniards' curse. Pride. I didn't want someone else telling me whom I should marry, right or wrong."

"And now?"

"And now," he pulled her closer, "I still have my pride, but my feeling for you makes it meaningless. I'm through running from you. Fighting bulls was just another way of running. Risking my life is no longer the fun or challenge it used to be because I have so very much to lose."

He brushed gently at her wet cheek. "Why the tears, my Analisa?"

She gave him a wobbly smile. "Because at last you're saying the words I've wanted so desperately to hear, and more beautifully than I could ever have imagined. Sometimes I think I've loved you forever."

"Even when we argued?"

"Especially then," she smiled. She took a deep breath and immediately felt dizzy.

Rafael looked at her in concern and put his arms around her. "What is it?"

She waited quietly for a moment until the spell passed, then gazed at Rafael with a look so filled with love that he gasped with the beauty of it. She took his strong brown hand and placed it gently on her abdomen. "Rafael, I'd like you to meet your child, who should arrive personally in about six and a half months."

He looked from her face to his hand, then back to her face. With a shout of joy, he lifted her into the air and swung her around, then carried her to the couch and sat down with her on his lap. "Shouldn't I offer you a cigar? I'm rather new at this sort of thing," he grinned.

"I think you do that *after* the birth—" She leaned back and sighed contentedly. "I wasn't really sure how you'd take the news of your impending parenthood."

"Why?"

"Oh, I don't really know. You were wonderful with the children at the school. I guess it was because I never heard you say you wanted some of your own."

He tilted her face toward his. "Perhaps that is because you are the only woman I have ever met with whom I have wanted to have children. With you, I knew they would all be children of love." He kissed her breathless, his lips moving over her shoulder and the gently rounded top of her breasts. His incredible blue eyes looked into her passion-glazed emerald ones. "Do you suppose our son or daughter would mind if we said hello properly to each other?"

"I can't imagine why," she said softly, knowing that this evening would be more special than any they had spent together so far. She knew he loved her.

He rose with her in his arms and started up the stairs. He stopped at the top and looked down at her. "I love you, my Analisa, and I am going to spend the rest of my life proving it to you."

Her arms tightened around his neck as he bent his head to kiss her smiling lips.

15-Day Free Trial Offer
6 Silhouette Romances

6 Silhouette Romances, free for 15 days! We'll send you 6 new Silhouette Romances to keep for 15 days, absolutely free! If you decide not to keep them, send them back to us. You pay nothing.

Free Home Delivery. But if you enjoy them as much as we think you will, keep them by paying the invoice enclosed with your free trial shipment. We'll pay all shipping and handling charges. You get the convenience of Home Delivery and we pay the postage and handling charge each month.

Don't miss a copy. The Silhouette Book Club is the way to make sure you'll be able to receive every new romance we publish before they're sold out. There is no minimum number of books to buy and you can cancel at any time.

This offer expires December 31, 1982

Silhouette Book Club, Dept SBQ 17B
120 Brighton Road, Clifton, NJ 07012

Please send me 6 Silhouette Romances to keep for 15 days, absolutely free. I understand I am not obligated to join the Silhouette Book Club unless I decide to keep them.

NAME_____

ADDRESS_____

CITY_____STATE_____ZIP_____

Silhouette Romance

IT'S YOUR OWN SPECIAL TIME

*Contemporary romances for today's women.
Each month, six very special love stories will be yours
from SILHOUETTE. Look for them wherever books are sold
or order now from the coupon below.*

$1.50 each

Hampson	☐ 1 ☐ 4 ☐ 16 ☐ 27 ☐ 28 ☐ 40 ☐ 52 ☐ 64 ☐ 94	Browning	☐ 12 ☐ 38 ☐ 53 ☐ 73 ☐ 93
Stanford	☐ 6 ☐ 25 ☐ 35 ☐ 46 ☐ 58 ☐ 88	Michaels	☐ 15 ☐ 32 ☐ 61 ☐ 87
Hastings	☐ 13 ☐ 26 ☐ 44 ☐ 67	John	☐ 17 ☐ 34 ☐ 57 ☐ 85
Vitek	☐ 33 ☐ 47 ☐ 66 ☐ 84	Beckman	☐ 8 ☐ 37 ☐ 54 ☐ 72 ☐ 96

$1.50 each

☐ 5 Goforth	☐ 29 Wildman	☐ 56 Trent	☐ 79 Halldorson
☐ 7 Lewis	☐ 30 Dixon	☐ 59 Vernon	☐ 80 Stephens
☐ 9 Wilson	☐ 31 Halldorson	☐ 60 Hill	☐ 81 Roberts
☐ 10 Caine	☐ 36 McKay	☐ 62 Hallston	☐ 82 Dailey
☐ 11 Vernon	☐ 39 Sinclair	☐ 63 Brent	☐ 83 Halston
☐ 14 Oliver	☐ 41 Owen	☐ 69 St. George	☐ 86 Adams
☐ 19 Thornton	☐ 42 Powers	☐ 70 Afton Bonds	☐ 89 James
☐ 20 Fulford	☐ 43 Robb	☐ 71 Ripy	☐ 90 Major
☐ 21 Richards	☐ 45 Carroll	☐ 74 Trent	☐ 92 McKay
☐ 22 Stephens	☐ 48 Wildman	☐ 75 Carroll	☐ 95 Wisdom
☐ 23 Edwards	☐ 49 Wisdom	☐ 76 Hardy	☐ 97 Clay
☐ 24 Healy	☐ 50 Scott	☐ 77 Cork	☐ 98 St. George
	☐ 55 Ladame	☐ 78 Oliver	☐ 99 Camp

$1.75 each

☐ 100 Stanford	☐ 105 Eden	☐ 110 Trent	☐ 115 John
☐ 101 Hardy	☐ 106 Dailey	☐ 111 South	☐ 116 Lindley
☐ 102 Hastings	☐ 107 Bright	☐ 112 Stanford	☐ 117 Scott
☐ 103 Cork	☐ 108 Hampson	☐ 113 Browning	☐ 118 Dailey
☐ 104 Vitek	☐ 109 Vernon	☐ 114 Michaels	☐ 119 Hampson

Silhouette Desire
15-Day Trial Offer

A new romance series
that explores
contemporary relationships
in exciting detail

Four Silhouette Desire romances, free for 15 days!
We'll send you four new Silhouette Desire romances
to look over for 15 days, absolutely free! If you decide
not to keep the books, return them and owe nothing.

Four books a month, free home delivery. If you like
Silhouette Desire romances as much as we think you
will, keep them and return your payment with the
invoice. Then we will send you four new books every
month to preview, just as soon as they are published.
You pay only for the books you decide to keep, and
you never pay postage and handling.

Silhouette Romance

Coming next month from
Silhouette Romances

Dreams From The Past by Linda Wisdom

Kelly went to Australia to fulfill a promise to her father, to see the woman he had first loved, Maureen Cassidy. How could she have known that in Maureen's son Jake she would find a love to last forever?

A Silver Nutmeg by Elizabeth Hunter

Judi Duggan had gone to Spain to design and stitch the trappings for the Arnalte family chapel. She didn't plan to meet the handsome Don—and she certainly didn't plan to fall in love!

Moonlight And Memories by Eleni Carr

Helen had dreamed of a chance to spend the summer in Greece. But the presence of deep, mysterious Demetrios Criades unsettled her. Could she unlock the passions hidden in the chambers of his heart?

Lover Come Back by Joanna Scott

One night of love made her his forever, bound by memory—and a child. Linda tried to escape, but how could she resist this master of the dangerous game of hearts?

A Treasure Of Love by Margaret Ripy

From the moment she met him, Marnie Stevens regretted signing on as Damon Wilson's underwater photographer. But with a will as steely as his penetrating gray eyes, he demanded fulfillment of the contract—in every way!

Lady Moon by Heather Hill

Maggie Jordan had come to the English countryside to restore Deane Park—a vast, Georgian estate. But after meeting its aristocratic owner, she realized the real challenge would be the man, not the job!